W9-BDH-509

A
Blossom
Promise

NOV 87

A Blossom Promise

BETSY BYARS

Illustrated by Jacqueline Rogers

DELACORTE PRESS/NEW YORK

NORTHPORT PUBLIC LIBRARY
NORTHPORT, NEW YORK

Published by
Delacorte Press
1 Dag Hammarskjold Plaza
New York, New York   10017

Text copyright © 1987 by Betsy Byars
Illustrations copyright © 1987 by Jacqueline Rogers

All rights reserved. No part of this book may be
reproduced or transmitted in any form or by any
means, electronic or mechanical, including
photocopying, recording or by any information storage
and retrieval system, without the written permission of
the Publisher, except where permitted by law.

Manufactured in the United States of America

First printing

Library of Congress Cataloging in Publication Data

Byars, Betsy Cromer.
  A Blossom promise.

  Summary: In the aftermath of a big flood in Alderson
County, a tragedy occurs and the Blossom family
continues coping in their rare family style.
  [1. Family life—Fiction.   2. Death—Fiction.
3. Grandfathers—Fiction]   I. Rogers, Jackie, ill.
II. Title.
PZ7.B9836Bh   1987   [Fic]   87-5367
ISBN 0-385-29578-2

Contents

A
Blossom
Promise

The Paper Bag

JUNIOR WAS PACKING A PAPER BAG. HE WISHED HE HAD a suitcase to pack, but he didn't and so he was putting just as much care into packing his paper bag. Junior was going to spend the night with Mad Mary.

In the bottom of the bag, neatly folded, was a pair of his mom's pajamas. Junior had to roll the pants legs up to keep from tripping over them, but it was the only nice pair of pajamas in the Blossom family.

On top of the pajamas was a Big Ben pad of paper and a pencil, in case he needed to do some writing. On top of that was his toothbrush, the family toothpaste, Maggie's comb, and a small broken mirror. On top of that was an extra pair of socks, his inch-long harmonica and two Snickers bars, one for him and one for Mary. Junior could tell which was which because he had already taken a bite out of his.

Junior stared at the contents for a moment and then, satisfied, he folded the top of the bag down neatly.

"I'm ready," he called happily.

Junior had been looking forward to spending the night

in Mad Mary's cave ever since the day he got to know her. Her cave was the most wonderful place Junior had ever been. It seemed to him like a museum display of cave life —full of strange plants, strange books, strange furniture, strange foods.

The best thing about the cave, to Junior, were the vultures that roosted above it. There was something about watching the huge birds making effortless circles in the morning sky that gave Junior a splendid, lighter-than-air feeling. It was such a special feeling that Junior wanted to know the name of it. He was looking forward to the day that particular feeling appeared in one of his spelling lists at school. He knew exactly how he would use the word in a sentence.

"When I see vultures in the sky," he would write, "I feel———."

Mad Mary had come personally to the Blossom farm to invite Junior. She had stood with one worn boot propped on the steps—she hadn't entered a house in seven years— and she yelled, "Junior!"

No one in the world sounded like Mad Mary. As the sound of her voice boomed through the house, Junior burst through the screen door.

"Junior," she said when he had calmed down, "I thought you were coming to spend the night."

"I was! I am!" he cried.

"When?"

"I don't know!" He turned to his grandfather in the doorway. "When, Pap? Saturday? Can I go this Saturday?"

"Saturday's fine," Pap had said.

"You'll bring him, Alec?"

"Nobody has to bring me, I'll—"

"I'll bring him."

"I'll be watching for you," Mary said. With a brisk nod, she had turned and disappeared into the woods.

But Saturday it had been raining, and it was still raining the next Saturday. The Catawba River crested on Sunday, and still it kept raining. Now Alderson County had had fourteen straight days of rain—a state record—and the whole county was flooded.

Every night "News at Eleven" showed pictures of residents riding down the county streets in boats instead of cars. Even Tom Brokaw, at 6:30, had called it the worst flood in the state's history.

Junior had begged to go that second Saturday despite the rain. "Why not?" he whined. "I was in her cave before when it rained."

"No, Junior," Pap said.

"I can take an umbrella."

"No."

"And wear boots."

"No!"

"If you don't want to take me, I'll go by myself. I know the way. I could get there blindfolded."

"Maybe you could, Junior, but when the valley gets underwater, there's lots of things you don't see. You step in what you think's a little puddle and it turns out to be a ten-foot hole. When the flood's over—"

"Pleeeeeease."

"Junior, your mom left me in charge—you heard her. The last thing she said was for you to mind me. So when I say no, it's no. And I say, 'No!' "

Now at last the rain had stopped. The sun was out. The mist that hung over the flooded fields had burned off.

3

People were out without umbrellas. The forecast was sunny and mild.

Normally Junior would be outside in the sunshine doing what everyone else in the county was doing—enjoying the flood. However, he had been wanting to go to Mary's for so long he couldn't get his mind on anything else.

"I'm ready," he called again.

He went through the living room and onto the front porch. "Paaaaap!" he called. Pap had promised to walk him to Mad Mary's right after lunch.

"Paaaaap!" Junior called again.

He could see that Pap's truck was still down by the creek, rammed sideways against an oak tree. At one point in the flooding, Pap had tried to drive the truck down the hill. The truck had slithered down the muddy slope like a sidewinder. If it hadn't rammed into the oak tree, it would have washed downstream.

Junior knew Pap had probably walked up the creek to admire the flooding. "But it's just water," Junior said to himself. "Why does it take so long to look at water?"

He sat on the steps and slumped dejectedly over his paper bag. "How can a plain old flood make him forget I was going to Mary's? Tell me that. How?" he asked the empty yard.

Junior felt water seep from the wet steps through his jeans, chilling his skin. He didn't care. He just wanted Pap to come home. He wanted to go!

He looked at his watch. It said, as it always did, 3:05. Junior thought it could be even later than that.

If Pap didn't get back soon, he wouldn't get to Mary's in time for supper. Mary would think he wasn't coming. She

4

would eat without him. All the varmint stew would be gone.

"Come on," Junior said. He gritted his teeth with impatience. "Come onnnnnn."

He rocked his feet back and forth on the step. Pap had once told him that every member of the Blossom family had restless feet. That was why they had joined the rodeo circuit in the first place. Junior knew now what Pap meant.

He scratched an old flea bite on his ankle. The minutes dragged by.

Junior sighed. Slowly he unfolded his paper bag and looked inside. To pass the time, he decided he would take one more bite of his Snickers bar. Carefully, as if he were peeling a banana, he folded back the paper.

As the smell of chocolate filled the air, Junior heard a noise under the porch. "Don't bother coming out, Dump," Junior told the dog. "I'm not sharing."

Dump came out into the strong sunlight blinking. His face was covered with spider webs and dirt.

"Don't give me pitiful looks," Junior said. Carefully he took one bite.

"You know I don't like to share candy bars. You've been my dog for," Junior paused to count, "eight months. That's long enough to know I don't like to share candy bars."

Dump kept sitting there, watching Junior, wagging his thin tail. His body wiggled with hope.

"Oh, all right."

Junior broke off a piece and gave it to Dump. Then he folded the paper around the rest and put it in the bag.

"Now that is it. Go back and chase frogs."

The flooding of the valley had brought a lot of frogs up to dry land. Some of them had taken refuge under the Blossoms' house. Junior could hear them croaking at night, their chorus louder at times than the roar of the creek.

As soon as Dump had discovered the frogs, he started spending a good part of his day jumping around the crawl space, pouncing on them. When he caught one in his mouth, he didn't know what to do with it and they always left a bitter taste. Still, he couldn't stop pouncing.

Junior leaned down and scratched Dump behind the ears. "I'm going to spend the night with Mary if Pap ever comes back."

Dump's eyes closed with pleasure as Junior's fingers scratched the spot that always itched. His tongue licked the air.

Junior's head snapped up. "Mary's probably sitting on her porch just like me—well, on the ledge in front of her cave. The ledge is her porch. She's probably sitting there right this minute. She's watching for me, wondering where I am. 'Where's Junior . . . ? What happened to Junior . . . ?' "

His look hardened.

"If Pap doesn't hurry and come back soon," he added, "I might just go without him."

The Raft

A MILE AWAY, UP SNAKE CREEK, VERN BLOSSOM AND HIS friend Michael were making a raft. Vern was whistling between his teeth. He always did this when he was happy. He had picked the habit up from Pap.

For the first time in his life, Vern had something to be proud of. It was always Junior who made things in the Blossom family and Vern who stood by and watched. Vern felt he had spent half of his life being an audience for Junior. Now, at last, he was making something. Junior would be the one to be astonished.

For one week, ever since the Catawba River crested and Snake Creek reached flood stage, Vern and Michael had been planning the raft. For one week they had collected logs and wood in the forest and scraps of rope and nails from their homes. They had stitched a sail in Michael's basement from a fitted bed sheet.

"Now don't tell anybody, all right?" Michael had said again and again. "They'll want to get in on it."

Vern always nodded instantly. He had no intention of

sharing his moment of greatness, his triumph, with anyone but his best friend.

"The raft will hold two people—max," Michael always went on. Michael couldn't work without talking. "Three people and it's . . ." He broke off at this point to hold his nose and pretend to sink under water. Then he added the real reason for silence, "Besides, if my mom found out . . ."

Vern had passed the week in a blaze of excitement. In school, he drew rafts in the margins of his papers, spending far more time on the nautical details than on his work. In the late afternoons, when Michael's mother called Michael into the house, Vern kept trudging tirelessly through the dripping forest, searching for raft material. At night, in his bed, unable to sleep from excitement, he closed his eyes and made the trip downstream in his mind.

The plan was simple. On the first Saturday after the rain, they would spend the morning assembling the raft. After lunch at approximately noon—"twelve bells," Michael called it—they would set out. The voyage would take them from Michael's house to Vern's, a nautical distance, they figured, of one mile.

Michael was not going to tell his family about the trip at all. Vern was going to tell Pap and Junior only that if they watched the creek carefully that afternoon, they would get the surprise of their lives.

As he and Michael sailed triumphantly down the creek on their raft, they would wave and shout at any neighbors who happened to be outside. Since the whole county was watching the creek, there was a good chance they would be seen and appreciated by a lot of people.

It was one of those events, Vern thought, that would go

9

down in county history. It would be talked about for years. "It was the year of the flood," storytellers would say in decades to come, "and the oldest Blossom boy—Vern—made a fine raft."

Every time Vern thought of the moment when he and Michael swept around the bend and into the startled gaze of Pap and Junior, two things happened. Goose bumps rose on his skinny arms, and a smile came over his face. At last he understood why Junior had smiled so much when he worked on his wings and his coyote trap and his Green Phantom.

"You made that raft?" Junior would say, incredulous.

"Of course."

"You made it?"

"Yes!"

And then, the inevitable, the completely satisfying final question. "Can I have a ride? Pleeeeeease!"

"We have to get finished today while the creek's still up real high," Michael said.

Vern nodded.

"If we have to wait till next Saturday, the creek might be back to normal. We'd get stuck on rocks and sand. It would be humiliating."

"I know." Vern and Michael had had the same conversations over and over, but neither had tired of them.

"And tomorrow I can't do it because I'll have on my Sunday clothes."

"Me too," Vern said. He could not remember ever owning clothes that exactly filled the description Sunday clothes, but he would have agreed to anything to get the raft afloat.

The boys were at the edge of the creek now. They had

spent the morning lashing logs together with rope. That was the underdeck, and it was finished.

Vern stepped back to admire their work. His foot slipped on the slick mud. He caught hold of a tree to steady himself. Then he glanced over his shoulder at the creek to see if there was any sign the water level was going down.

Michael read his thoughts. "My dad says the creek won't go down for a week." Michael was wiping his hands off on his overalls. He was getting ready to use his father's hammer.

"That's what Pap says too," Vern said.

"But we can't count on that. I mean, we can't say, 'Well, if we don't finish today, we can do it next Saturday or the Saturday after that.' "

"No," Vern agreed.

He let go of the tree. He bent to give one of the knots a closer inspection. The ends of the knot were cut too short. It might untie under the pressure of the voyage.

"You got any more rope in your bag?" he asked Michael. "I don't trust some of these knots."

Michael checked his paper bag. "No, you?"

"No." Vern didn't have to check his. He knew that all he had left was a handful of bent nails. "But," he added, "I know where some vines are."

"Would vines work?"

"They better."

Michael grinned. "Let's go," he said. He put down the hammer and pulled his hunting knife from its leather sheath.

Vern pulled out his knife too. Vern's was one of his mother's kitchen knives, but Vern had made a case like

Michael's out of cardboard. He had laced the edges together with brown twine. In his own eyes, the knives and cases were identical.

Brandishing their knives, whooping for joy, the boys ran for the woods.

The Grand Entry

MAGGIE BLOSSOM WAS HUNDREDS OF MILES AWAY. SHE was on her mother's horse Sandy Boy, and she was lined up for the grand entry of the 61st annual Tucson rodeo.

Ahead of her was a long shifting line of horses and people—the color guard with their flags snapping in the wind, the rodeo princesses, the officials, the other Wrangler Riders. At the end of the line were two clowns; one was riding a zebra, the other a mule.

Maggie could hear the whinnying of horses from the open stalls, the bawling of calves. The warm, dusty air smelled of beer, popcorn, and hot dogs.

Over the loudspeaker, the announcer was doing the pre-show, the junior rodeo. A groan came from the crowd as one of the kids missed in the calf roping.

"That's too bad, folks," the announcer said. "He threw the loop where the money would have been. Tough luck, Randy. Let's pay him off, folks." The crowd clapped as Randy ran for the gate.

Maggie shifted in the saddle. Her mom glanced around

at her and grinned. She tugged the brim of her hat. Maggie did the same.

Vicki Blossom was on a yellow horse named Traveler. She had borrowed Traveler so Maggie could have Sandy Boy. "You're used to Sandy Boy," Vicki had told her, "I can ride anything."

Ahead of Vicki Blossom were the other four Wrangler Riders. They wore matching white satin shirts, white hats, white boots, and skin-tight Wrangler jeans. They were the five best trick riders in the United States.

The announcer was winding up the junior rodeo events. "How about a hand of applause for the cowboys and cowgirls of the Arizona Junior Rodeo Association? Thank you. We sure do enjoy showing off our youngsters here in Arizona.

"And now, folks, at the southern gate is Joe Nevada, Rodeo Announcer of the Year, who'll be announcing all the exciting action of the Tucson Rodeo on horseback. Let's put our hands together and give him an Arizona welcome!"

Maggie took in a deep breath. This was it, the day she had been waiting for. Today she would be riding with the Wrangler Riders in front of thousands of people. Beneath her white satin shirt, her heart was beating twice as fast as usual. She licked her dry lips. She settled her white hat more securely on her head.

Over the loudspeaker, Joe Nevada was asking the crowd to draw in a big breath of clear, warm Tucson air and let it out in a whoop and a holler. There was a lusty yell from the crowd, and Mrs. Blossom glanced around at Maggie. She tugged her hat again; that was a kind of signal. She said, "Here we go, shug."

14

The band struck up "Hey, Look Me Over." The gate opened. The grand entry began.

Sandy Boy had been in so many rodeo parades, so many grand entries, he could probably have done it blindfolded. But, for Maggie, it had been a long, long time, of waiting and practicing. This grand entry was something special.

When Maggie was little, she used to ride in front of her mom in all the grand entries. "Smile, shug," her mother was always saying. "Don't be so serious."

People used to point them out as Vicki and Maggie rode around the rodeo grounds together. "That's Cotton's wife and kid," they said. "Do you mind if we take your picture?"

"We'd be proud," Vicki always answered.

There was a newspaper picture of the two of them in the family scrapbook. There was no date, but the caption was "Vicki Blossom and daughter Maggie. Vicki will be doing trick riding this weekend at the rodeo. Her daughter is rodeo mascot." Even being rodeo mascot had not made Maggie smile. "You look as solemn as an owl," her mother said when she saw the picture.

But this rodeo was different. She would not be riding in front of her mom. She would not be a mascot. She was on her own, and as far as Maggie was concerned this was the beginning of her new life. For the first time, people were actually treating her like an adult.

The procession wove around the arena. Striped flags snapped over the grandstands. The crowd cheered. The horses pranced. The procession ended with all the horses and riders side by side, facing the crowd.

"And now," Joe Nevada said in a more serious voice, "while our flag is carried around the arena, let's stand.

15

This beautiful banner was a gift from God. We think of the many places she's been we didn't want her to be and we thank her for over two hundred years of freedom. And now the number one song in the national hit parade, the National Anthem!"

Some of the horses were sidestepping, nervously prancing in place, but not Sandy Boy. Maggie leaned forward and patted his neck.

Out of the corner of her eye, she saw that the other Wranglers had their hats off and their hands over their hearts. Quickly Maggie did the same.

Then, too soon for Maggie, the grand entry was over and the procession was leaving the arena. The Wrangler Riders would be coming back to perform between the bareback riding and the steer wrestling events.

Maggie paused in the sunshine to catch her breath. Behind her the gate had closed. The bareback riding event was under way.

The announcer was saying, "The handle they use is about the size of a suitcase handle, folks, but that's where the likeness ends, 'cause I don't think your average suitcase weighs fifteen hundred pounds and jumps around on the end of your arm."

The crowd laughed.

"Let's go now to the bucking chutes. First up is Pete Dobler on Jr. Garrison. Here he comes, folks."

Vicki Blossom rode up beside Maggie. "I was nervous," Maggie admitted.

"You?"

Maggie nodded.

"Why on earth would you be nervous? You been doing this all your life."

16

"It's different now," Maggie said, "I'm different now."

"Well, no daughter of mine's going to be nervous. You can be excited if you want to, but that's it."

"All right," Maggie said, "I'm excited."

Behind them the crowd groaned. The announcer was saying, "—down too soon and he left out the back door. Back door, side door, it don't matter as long as you get out before the house burns down. Let's pay him off, folks."

There was applause. "In about fifteen minutes," her mom pointed at her, "that applause will be for you."

"Oh, Mom."

"It will. Smile, shug. Don't be so serious. We're having fun!"

The Thing Under the Porch

"PAAAAAAAP!"

Junior was leaning forward despondently. Both elbows were pressing into his paper bag suitcase.

"Why doesn't he come on home?" he asked Dump. "Where is he?"

Junior glanced down. He noticed for the first time that Dump was no longer there listening to him. Dump had gone back under the house to pester the frogs.

"Just go off and leave me, Dump, I don't care," Junior said. "Everybody in this whole family can go off and leave when they want to but me." His voice was deep with pity and resentment.

He began to list his grievances. "Vern didn't have to wait for Pap to take him to Michael's. Pap didn't have to have special permission to go down the creek. Neither did Mud. You go under the house every time you want a frog. I am the only Blossom who has to have permission."

He made a scornful face to show what he thought of permission. He wished every single one of them had been there to see it.

Junior heard a heavy thud as Dump's head struck the floorboards, then a yelp of pain. Every now and then Dump would get so intent on the frogs, he would forget he was under the house and rear up like a horse.

"That's what you get," Junior said wisely.

In the silence that followed, Junior added, "Anyway, you better leave those frogs alone, Dump. Their juice is poison. Pap told me so. That's why your mouth foams so much when you catch one."

Junior went back to feeling sorry for himself.

He said, "Pap knows I'm going to spend the night with Mary. I've been waiting and waiting to do this and now Pap just goes off. He doesn't care whether I get to go or not. He only cares about the flooooood." Another scornful face.

Junior rolled his eyes down to where the swollen creek roared, rushing to the sea. Normally this would have been a great adventure for Junior. The creek had never been this high in his lifetime.

And not only that, but all kinds of interesting trash was coming down with the flood—boards, buckets, wooden crates, old tires. Junior should have been down on the bank, pulling in these things, storing them in the barn for his next invention.

Junior watched as a garbage pail lid swirled into sight. A flicker of interest came to his eyes, but he shook it off. The only thing in the whole world that he wanted was to go to Mary's.

"Paaaaaaaap! Come onnnnnnnnn!" Junior yelled. "Are you ever coming?"

Junior glanced down at his paper bag. It was as flat now as an old pillow. He plumped it back into shape.

19

Then, slowly, he unfolded the top. He had done this so many times that the top had fringes.

With squinted eyes, he took in the contents. The only thing he could seem to see anymore was his Snickers bar. He gave a long, regretful sigh.

He reached down into the bag and his fingers curled around the candy bar. He didn't want to be doing this, but he couldn't stop himself. He pulled it out slowly.

He unwrapped it for the fourth time. There was only one inch of candy left. Junior turned it sideways and bit off half, leaving a small cube of candy. At least it looked nice and square, Junior thought, like something out of a box of chocolates. He wished he had one of those little frilled paper cups to set it in. Well, he didn't.

He folded the cube up in the wrapper and put it in his paper bag. Junior no longer thought of his paper bag as a suitcase. It was too out of shape.

"Now," he said firmly, as he had done several times since he took his seat on the porch steps, "I am not going to eat any more of my candy bar *no matter what.* If I do, I won't have anything for a snack tonight. Mary will be eating her candy, and I'll just have to sit there. She would offer me some of hers probably, but—"

Just thinking about sitting beside Mary, candy-less, watching her enjoy her candy bar, made him throw back his head in anguish.

"Pap! Pleeeeease! Pleeeeeease come home!"

Dump's ears went back up. He had now recovered from hitting himself on the head and was ready for more action.

A frog jumped beside him and Dump swirled. He reached out with one paw.

To Dump's surprise, the move was successful. The frog was pinned to the ground.

Dump spent a moment enjoying the feel of the frog throbbing softly beneath his paw. Then he bent and gingerly took the frog by one leg. He held him for a moment, dangling in the air, as if he weren't quite sure what he wanted to do next.

The frog jerked and Dump snapped at him. The snapping motion brought the frog into Dump's mouth. There was a brief moment of satisfaction, and then Dump's mouth was filled with the bitter liquid he hated.

He dropped the frog and shook his head to get rid of the terrible taste. Spit flew. Dump shook his head again. His long ears flapped around his head.

"Pleeeeease!" Junior begged above him.

Dump shook his head again. The bitter taste was almost bearable, and Dump looked down at the frog. The frog sat where he had been dropped. Dump watched him. Dump liked a moving target. He scratched the earth behind the frog, trying to provoke him into action. The frog did not move, and Dump lay down to wait it out.

"Pleeeeeeease!" Junior yelled louder.

Dump lifted his head. He had just seen something. Something in the distance, in the shadows around the chimney, had moved. Tail up, Dump got to his feet.

For a long moment he watched. He didn't even seem to be breathing. Then slowly he began to move toward the chimney.

He took three steps. He went into a hunter's crouch. His front legs trembled with excitement.

He was close enough now to smell the creature, and it

21

did not smell like frog. He took three more steps. He stopped beside an old faded wooden crate.

Dump's ears were pulled together in puzzlement. He had never seen anything like this before. He had never smelled anything like this either. He sat down tensely on his haunches to watch.

It was not a frog. It was long and coiled, and it watched Dump with bright, slitted eyes that never blinked.

In a crouch, Dump left the apple crate and moved forward. He was five feet away from his target now.

He pawed the ground again. Dump had long coltlike legs, and his movements were often more like a horse than a dog.

Still the long, coiled thing did not move. Dump went one step closer. He pawed the earth again. The long, coiled thing watched him with unwavering eyes.

Above him, on the porch, Junior yelled, "Pull-eeease!" one last anguished time, but Dump was too intent on this thing under the porch to hear.

Up the Creek Without a Paddle

"MICHAEL, WHERE ARE YOU GOING?"

Michael and Vern stopped in their tracks. They were at the kitchen door of Michael's house. Vern had been reaching for the doorknob. His mud-stained hand froze in the air. Beside him, Michael swallowed aloud.

"Nowhere, Mom," he said.

"Michael . . ."

"Mom, we were just going outside."

"What's that behind your back?"

"Nothing."

"I don't like that kind of answer."

Vern did not look at Michael's mother. Vern did what he always did around Mrs. McMann. He watched the floor. He was familiar with all the floors in Michael's house. He could not remember the color of any of the walls or the furniture, but he knew the floors. This was the artificial brick Congoleum.

Even though he was watching the floor, Vern knew, from the cold silence that followed, exactly what Mrs. McMann's expression would be—disapproving. Nobody

24

could say, "I don't like that answer," better than Michael's mom. She turned it into a double accusation—she made Michael feel bad for giving the answer and Vern for somehow inspiring it.

"Michael," his mother prompted.

She took off her glasses. This was even more ominous. Vern felt she could see directly into their minds without the protective tinted glass.

Slowly Michael brought the paddle out from behind his back.

"That's the paddle to your father's pontoon boat, isn't it?"

"Yes."

"What were you planning to do with it?"

Both of the boys were watching the floor now. Michael did not answer.

"Look at me, Michael."

Vern was glad he didn't have to look at her. Even if she had demanded that he do so, he wasn't sure he could.

"You boys were not planning to put your father's boat in the creek, were you?" There was genuine horror in her voice now.

"No, ma'am!" Michael said emphatically. He met his mother's look with equal horror. His voice rose with shock and relief. "Dad told us never to use the boat without him."

"Yes, but—"

"I would never take the boat without permission. I promise. I only wanted the paddle. Mom, that's the truth. I would never—"

"I believe you, Michael."

There was another silence. Vern waited, shoulders

hunched tensely for the next question. It would be, "Then what were you going to do with the paddle?"

When Michael answered it—and Michael didn't lie to his mother—then the trip down the river would be over. Michael would not be allowed to go, and neither would he.

Michael's mother often said, "Now, Vern, your mother would not want you to do that." Vern had stopped saying, "She doesn't care what I do, Mrs. McMann! Honest!" because that answer seemed especially displeasing.

"Vern," Michael's mother said.

Vern shut his eyes. His shoulders got ready to take a hard blow.

"What have you got behind your back?"

"Me?"

He looked up, as surprised by his question as Michael had been.

"Yes."

Vern brought out a can of Mello Yellow. He had instinctively hidden it because he and Michael were going to use it to christen the raft. Vern knew Michael's mother would somehow sense that this was not just a normal can of pop, that it was going to be used for something she would not approve of.

To his surprise, Michael's mother actually smiled.

"Can we go now?" Michael asked quickly, seizing the opportunity of a lifetime—that was how it seemed to Vern anyway.

"Yes, you can go."

Both boys turned to the door. Vern's muddy fingers curled around the doorknob.

"Only, Michael—"

Both boys stopped.

"Put the paddle back where you got it."

"Yes'm."

"I'll wait outside," Vern said quickly. He rushed out of the house. He stood in the middle of the yard, gulping in the clean, fresh air like a man just out of prison.

Vern was still standing there, breathing through his mouth, when Michael joined him. "Anyway," Michael said, "we can get along without the paddle. All we really needed it for was to make sure we ended up on your side of the creek. Boards will do. I mean, we don't have to paddle our way down the creek or anything. That's what floods are for."

Vern turned to Michael, and he used an old expression of Pap's. "I thought we were goners," he said.

The Floating Shoes

"MUD, NOW THAT'S WHAT I CALL A FLOOD," PAP SAID.

Pap was standing at the edge of Snake Creek, watching the water sweep around the grove of willow trees.

"Right over there is where you and me sit and fish." He shook his head. "Only our rock is five feet under water. No telling what the fish think about all this."

Pap turned to look down the creek. Again he shook his head.

Beyond the willow trees, the creek left its banks entirely and took a shortcut through the Edwards' field. The whole pasture was under water. Only the tips of the fence posts stuck up, and the barbwire between was strung with trash. The Angus cows had been moved to higher ground.

"You're never going to see more water than this in your whole life, Mud. The valley's more water now than it is land."

Pap's old eyes shone. From the time he was a boy, Pap had had a fascination with water. He'd almost drowned four times before he reached the age of ten.

He had just finished telling Mud about the first time—

he was one year old and he fell into the toilet which his family had just gotten installed. It was the first indoor toilet in the history of the Blossom family, so naturally it was a fascinating thing to all of them.

If his mother hadn't heard the splash and come in saying, "Alec, if you're playing in the toilet again, I'm going to wear you out," well, he wouldn't be here today.

Now, as he and Mud started around the flooded pasture, he began telling about his second near-drowning. Mud broke away to take a shortcut. He ran through the shallow water, his long legs glistening in the sunlight.

Pap kept walking slowly, taking the long way around, the way that favored bad knees.

"Mud, I had a brother Jess that was a lot like Junior," Pap said, even though Mud was too far away to hear him now. "Jess would make things, only he wouldn't test them himself the way Junior does. He had better sense. He'd get us, his little brothers, to test them. I was the water man. If it had anything to do with water, then Jess would offer it to me."

Mud ran back. He leaped nimbly over a fallen tree. Pap climbed over, holding on with both hands. He sat for a moment on the wet wood, giving his knees a rest.

"One time it was floating shoes. Jess swore I could walk clear across the pond and not even get wet if I'd put them on."

Mud circled back around the clearing with his nose to the ground, on the scent of something. Pap got up slowly and started walking.

"I put up a little struggle, but I ended up letting him tie the fool things on my feet. They was innertubes folded in half with my feet tied in the middle.

29

"Well, I went out on the dock where we fished. The floating shoes was big clumsy things, but I knew they'd float because they were blowed up tight."

Mud paused at the foot of a large tree. He looked up intently into the dripping branches. His look sharpened. His ears flopped back. In a bound he put his paws on the trunk and let out a piercing bark.

"What is it Mud? Possum?"

That was Mud's attack word. Whenever Pap used it—whether he was pointing to a hole in the ground with his boot or a cat in a tree, Mud knew what was expected of him.

Now he began leaping excitedly up the trunk of the tree. His high, shrill barks rang through the afternoon air, above the roar of the creek.

Pap looked up the tree. "Well, it is a possum for once, Mud."

Pap watched the possum. It was a miserable ball of wet fur curled in the shelter of a forked limb.

"He probably got flooded out of his home. We won't give him any more misery than he's already got. Let's let him be, Mud."

Mud did not obey immediately. Pap had to say "Let him be" one more time before it had the desired effect.

Mud got down reluctantly. "Good dog," Pap said. As they started around the field, side by side now, Pap took up his story.

"Well, Mud, I went out there on the dock, waddling like a duck. I was just going to take a few steps with my brothers holding me, but soon as I got my feet on the water, they let go."

The memory caused Pap to pause for a moment, drawn

back in time. He put out his arms the way he had that July Sunday, then he shook his head.

"Oh, them shoes floated all right, Mud. Jess was right about that. They floated. Only I didn't. I was turned upside down in two seconds flat.

"My brothers never were ones to do the smart thing. They went running to the house, yelling 'Mama, Alec's drowning!' If they knowed I was drowning—which I was—why didn't they jump in?

"I couldn't hear none of this. I was too busy holding my breath. Well, my mother dove in wearing her Sunday dress and an apron. It was the first time she was ever known to go in water willingly. My brothers dove in too—and then the hired man came up and saw everybody jumping in and he jumped in too. Between the five of them they turned me right side up or I'd not be walking along the creek today."

Pap paused again to watch the creek. "This is the worst flood in the history of the state. If the rain had gone on, let's see"—he paused to figure it out—"twenty-two more days, it would have been as bad as the flood in the Bible.

"Everywhere you look, Mud"—he turned his head to take it all in—"there's fine old fields covered with water, chickens floating away on pieces of chicken houses, trees that I've leaned on for years looking like they could use my help now.

"I tell you, Mud, if this creek don't stop rising soon, there ain't going to be no more valley."

The Wrangler Riders

THERE WAS ONLY ONE CONTESTANT LEFT IN THE SADDLE
bronc riding event, but the announcer was reminding the
crowd, "It ain't over till it's over, folks, and here in chute
number eight is Spitfire.

"Folks," he went on, "this horse does everything right
except that his clutch slips. Here he comes! It's a snappy
ride. It's a good one! . . . That's a sixty-seven score for
Scooter. Let's pay them all off, folks."

There was applause for all the bronc riders. The applause grew louder as the winner came in and raised his
hat to the crowd.

Maggie was waiting at the south end of the arena, behind the gate, with the other Wrangler Riders. The winner of the bronc riding event went back to the chutes.

Then the gate opened, and Maggie's heart stopped
beating. Beyond the other Wrangler Riders she could see
the arena . . . the crowd . . .

"And now, ladies and gentlemen," Joe Nevada said,
"the Sixty-first Annual Tucson Rodeo is proud to present

the Wrangler Riders. This is a thank you from Wrangler to all of their many customers over the years."

The band began to play. The music was so fast, so furious, Maggie couldn't even tell what the song was. The first Wrangler Rider—B.B.—kicked her horse, let out a war whoop, and rode into the arena.

B.B.'s specialty was Indian riding. She went around the arena as fast as the music. As she passed the grandstand, she dropped under her horse, came up on the other side. On her second pass she hit the ground and vaulted back on her horse. The crowd burst into cheers.

"And now, folks," the announcer said, "here's Sadie the Lady Williams."

Sadie came into the arena riding two horses; both of them were black. She rode gladiator style, with one foot on one horse, one on the other. As she passed the grandstand, she stepped onto one horse and raised her hat. On her second pass she jumped nimbly back and forth. The roar from the crowd filled the air again.

"We're proud to have Vicki Blossom back with us today. We've missed her. Here she comes, folks. Let's give her a rodeo welcome home."

Vicki Blossom did a headstand on her first pass. Maggie watched her from the gate.

Maggie's heart had moved up and lodged in her throat. She couldn't swallow. She tried to wet her lips and tasted dust. The blood was pumping so hard in her neck she could hear it above the roar of the crowd.

Her mother was back at the gate. Her horse reared. "Come on, shug," she said to Maggie. Maggie dug her heels into Sandy Boy.

In a daze she heard the words of the announcer. "La-

33

dies and gentlemen, we got a three-generation cowgirl with the Wranglers this afternoon—Maggie Blossom. Her granddad was Alec Blossom, the best rope twirler I've ever seen, her dad was Cotton Blossom, a world champion, and that's her proud mom, Vicki Blossom, on the yellow horse."

Maggie and her mom went around the arena, side by side. On their first pass, they hooked their knees over the saddle horn and dropped off the side of the horses. On the second pass, they did shoulder stands.

The blood rushed to Maggie's head. The arena, the grandstands whirled around her. The whole world was a blur of color and noise.

Then, before she knew it, all the Wrangler Riders were in the arena, riding around, whooping, doing one trick after another. On the last pass, they all hooked their knees around their saddles and dropped off the backs of their horses. They raised their hats to the crowd as they left the arena.

The announcer said, "Let's put our hands together and show all the Wrangler Riders what we think of them."

"It was over so quick," Maggie said to her mother when she was out of the arena and right-side-up. They started riding for the stables, side by side. Maggie's face was flushed with excitement.

"I know—five minutes in the arena always does seem like five seconds."

B.B. pulled up beside them. "You did great, Maggie," she said.

"Thanks."

She said, "You're going to be better than your old lady one of these days."

"Now, now, let's don't get carried away," Vicki said, laughing.

Maggie laughed too. She unsaddled Sandy Boy as her mom and the other Wrangler Riders unsaddled their horses. From the arena they could hear applause, shouts, groans of sympathy, Joe Nevada's enthusiastic "Boy, I like this one, we got one going, folks."

"I'm just going to hate to leave all this and go home, Mom," Maggie said.

"But you got to go to school. The only way you got to come at all was because of spring break."

"I know."

"Still, I guess it wouldn't hurt you to miss one week of school."

"What do you mean, Mom?"

"I mean I'm going to let you stay another week. The school won't care. I'll give you a note saying you were sick."

"Mom, will you really?"

"Yes, and anyway, Maggie, it'll be summer before long. We'll all be together on the circuit. Our lives will just be one long rodeo."

B.B. passed behind Sandy Boy. She grinned at Vicki and winked. "Bull riding's coming up, Vicki," she said. "You sure don't want to miss that."

"B.B.," Vicki said. She glanced at Maggie in a warning way.

Maggie looked at her mother. "I thought you never watched the bull riding anymore, you said you couldn't, not after what happened to Daddy."

"Well, I couldn't for a long time," Vicki Blossom said quickly. "I still can't hardly watch it, but I'm getting better about it. I tell you what. Let's both watch it today, want to?" She put one arm around Maggie and glanced at B.B. over Maggie's head. "Some people," she said, "ought to learn to keep their big mouths shut."

The Queen

"WHAT DO YOU WANT TO CALL IT?" VERN ASKED MI-chael.

"I don't know. What do you want to call it?"

"I don't know. I asked you first."

Vern and Michael had now nailed the last plank into place. The raft was finished. It was at the edge of the water, ready to be launched with one good push.

The raft was the most beautiful thing Vern had ever seen. He had always enjoyed making small things, and in the past he had often made little rafts because twigs and vines were mainly what he had to work with.

He had spent a lot of time on those little rafts, making sure they were seaworthy before sending them down the creek, imagining them reaching the ocean, bobbing in the ripples of the tide. All those dozens of tiny rafts seemed now to have been working models for this—the real thing. He had been a scientist perfecting his craft, and now here it was, a reality at last.

The only thing left to do was give it a name.

"I'm not good with names," Michael admitted. "That's

why I get bad grades in English. I can write the stories, but I can't give them names. Mr. Levy won't even read it if he sees 'A Story' on the top."

"Well, I can't name stories either."

The boys stood in silence for a moment, watching their creation beside the rushing waters. The one thing they both knew was that it was beautiful, and it deserved an impressive name.

The base of the raft was made of the logs they had found in the woods and carried, one boy on each end, to the creek. The top was a deck of boards. The boards were all different shapes and sizes, some new boards, some gray and weathered. The boards overlapped—it gave a sort of shingled look, and the boys figured the water would flow over the boards the way rain ran down a shingled roof.

The effect was one of unity, harmony, great beauty, and —the boys thought—strength.

At the back of the raft was the mast and the bed-sheet sail. The sail was mostly for decoration, but it was already flapping briskly in the breeze, raising the level of excitement, giving the boys the feeling that the voyage was already under way.

"Why has it got to have a name?" Michael asked. "Why couldn't it just be the raft?" With his fingers he put quotation marks around the last two words.

"It's got to have a name. Like, remember, Junior's UFO was the Green Phantom? Anyway, boats always have names." This was important to Vern. Years from now he wanted to be able to remember it by name.

Michael sensed this was important to Vern. He said, "I saw a special on TV about a raft, but I can't remember the name or we could use that. It was foreign."

38

"Our name should be American."

"How about . . ." Michael paused. "Now, remember I'm not very good at names."

"Me either."

"Then how about this. The USS *Mayflower*. You can't get any more American than that."

"Yes, it's American all right."

Vern scratched his head with his dynamited finger. The end of the finger had been blown off one time when Vern was investigating a small black cylinder which turned out to be a blasting cap. Whenever Vern scratched his head with his dynamited finger, Vern was deep in thought.

Finally Vern said, "I don't know. It's too—naval or something, too old-timey maybe."

"Well, I told you I wasn't good at names," Michael said.

"How about something like . . ." Vern paused to swallow. He had had this name in mind all morning, but he wanted to wait until the last minute to spring it. He looked off into the distance, trying to appear deep in thought.

He let his face light up, as if the idea had just that second popped into his mind. "How about the Queen?" he said.

"Say it again."

"The Queen. You know, like the Mississippi Queen or the Delta Queen. Ours will just be the Queen."

"It's okay, I guess," Michael said.

"If you don't like it . . ."

"No, it's fine," Michael said impatiently. "It's perfect! Get the Mello Yellow."

Vern reached into the bib of his overalls, where he had put the can for safekeeping. The can had left a cold spot on his chest. He handed the can to Michael, and Michael pulled the tab.

Vern would have liked the honor of christening the raft himself, but he didn't want to be a hog—naming the raft and christening it too.

"I christen thee the Queen," Michael said. He poured a little Mello Yellow onto the upper deck.

The boys stood in silence for a moment, awed by the official words they had previously heard only on TV or at the movies.

It was Michael who broke the spell. He took a gulp of Mello Yellow, burped, and passed the can to Vern. Vern drank, burped, and passed the can back to Michael.

The can went back and forth until it was empty. At that point, Vern wiped his hands on the bib of his overalls.

"Now," he said, "let's push the Queen into the water and get going."

Junior's Journey

JUNIOR GOT UP FROM THE STEPS. HE STUFFED HIS SUIT-case under his arm.

"I've had it," he said.

He glanced down at his watch. The hands still pointed to 3:05.

"I will wait exactly three more minutes and then I'm leaving. That is my final word."

Junior closed his eyes so he could concentrate on count-ing out the minutes. Since his watch didn't work—it had said 3:05 since the day Junior found it in the Sears parking lot and strapped it on his arm—Junior had developed his own method of counting time.

Junior's way was to close his eyes and stand absolutely still until he thought three minutes was up. Then he would keep standing there until he thought another three minutes was up. That worked out fine. Minutes were ex-actly twice as long as most people thought.

When both three minutes were up, Junior opened his eyes. Pap wasn't in sight, so Junior said, "That's it."

He went into the house. He crossed the hall and en-

41

tered the kitchen. He breathed air that smelled of the fried egg sandwiches Pap had fixed that morning.

Junior thought that Pap and Mad Mary were the best cooks in the world. Both of them put a lot of originality into their cooking. Mary did it with possum and onions, Pap with bacon grease.

Junior thought that very few cooks would take their sandwiches and, just before serving them, toss them into hot bacon grease for a few seconds. A lot of people in this world—and not just people overseas either—had never even tasted a fried sandwich. At least that's what Pap said, and Junior believed him.

Junior looked around the kitchen counter, but he couldn't find a sheet of paper, so he took a brown paper bag, folded it, and wrote. "I have gone to Mary's. Don't worry. I know the way by heart." He signed it "Love to all, Junior."

He propped the note on the table, like a tent, and went back out onto the porch. He adjusted his paper bag suitcase under his arm. He was leaving—that was definite, but while he was going, he would give Pap every chance in the world to put in an appearance.

He took the steps one by one, like a small child. In a sort of processional way—pause—step—pause—step, he crossed the soggy yard.

At the edge of the forest, his head snapped up. His head always went up like a flag when he had a brilliant thought. This was Junior's thought—the horn on Pap's truck.

Junior hit himself on the head. "You should have thought of that an hour ago." He ran down the hill to where Pap's truck leaned against the oak tree. The truck was sideways, so Junior had a hard time getting the door open. He slid into the driver's seat. He leaned on the horn.

One long, two shorts. This was Pap's signal to Mud when he wanted to go somewhere. Junior repeated the signal. Beeeeeep. Beep. Beep.

He leaned back to wait.

It was steaming hot in the truck. The truck had been shut up for days. Junior wiped his dripping brow.

He sat forward and gave the signal one more time. Beeeeeep. Beep. Beep. He leaned up to look out the windshield. He glanced up the creek and down. Slowly, the smile faded on his face. He climbed out of the truck and jumped down onto the soft wet earth.

That was it, Junior decided. He would go to Mary's by himself.

His head snapped up. Another brilliant thought.

He would go to Mary's, but not by himself. He would take Dump along. Then if Pap got mad, he could say, "I knew you didn't want me to go by myself, and I didn't. I took Dump."

Well, one thing was working out. He would not have to look for Dump. Dump was under the house with the frogs.

"I'll crawl under," Junior told himself, "pull him out, and be on my way."

He ran up the hill.

"Dump," he called happily. "Good news! You and me are going somewhere really fun! We're going to Mary's!"

Clutching his paper bag suitcase, Junior ran to the house.

Beeeeeep. Beep. Beep.
Pap stopped in his tracks.

43

He had just heard the sound of his truck's horn. It was the signal he used to let Mud know he was ready to go.

Pap lifted his head with sudden thought.

"Oh, Mud, that's Junior," he said. "That is Junior."

The new tone of Pap's voice made Mud stop too. Mud turned to see if anything was wrong.

"Yes, Mud, something is wrong," Pap said, reading his mind. "We clean forgot about Junior."

Mud watched Pap, his ears drawn together, his brow wrinkled.

"I promised to take him to Mary's. Come on, Mud, we got to get home. Junior is going to be mighty unhappy with us."

Pap turned. As he began retracing his steps, he called, "I'm coming, Junior, I'm coming."

He knew he was too far away for Junior to hear him, but it made him feel better.

To Mud he said, "I'll have to tell you about the third time I almost drowned some other time."

Mud did not move.

Pap knew that Mud still had hopes of continuing on down the creek, seeing new sights, smelling new ground. Otherwise Mud would have passed him. Mud was always the leader on their walks.

Pap stopped and turned. Mud was standing still, watching him. His golden eyes were bright with hope.

"I know you want to keep going," Pap said. "I know you want to see what's around the bend. I do too. Only, Mud, we got to go home and keep a promise to Junior."

Pap started for home, and then, tail wagging, Mud bounded after him.

45

The Trouble with the Voyage

❧   ❧   ❧

"ONE . . . TWO . . ." VERN STOPPED COUNTING.

He and Michael were bent over, waiting for the "three . . . Go!" so they could push the raft into the creek. Instead of finishing the countdown, Vern straightened.

"What's wrong?" Michael asked.

"Nothing."

"Then why did you stop counting?"

"Well, I just remembered something. Before we go, I want to go up to your house and use your phone, all right? I want to call Junior and Pap so they'll be out in the yard to see us land."

"Mom will hear you," Michael warned.

"Not if I use the phone in your dad's workshop."

"She'll hear you no matter what phone you use. She has twenty-twenty hearing. Last night, I was in the kitchen and I said, 'Idiot,' to my brother, which you know he is, and my mom was up in the bedroom with the door shut, running the sewing machine, and she yelled, 'Apologize to your brother. I won't have you calling your brother names.'"

"But if I don't call," Vern said, "they might not be outside. They might not even see us."

"But if you do call and my mom hears you, we won't get to go, period."

Vern paused, lost in thought. He scratched his head with his dynamited finger.

"On the other hand," Michael went on. He had been doing some thinking himself. "If you don't call and they aren't out there, and if we get in trouble, then there won't be anybody to help us."

Vern looked quickly at Michael. "What kind of trouble did you have in mind?"

"All kinds!"

"Like?"

Michael glanced down at his feet.

"Like what kind of trouble?"

"Well, like landing, for instance."

"You're worried about landing?"

"Yes, frankly, I am. I mean, sure, we'll land somewhere. I just want to make sure it's at your house. And not only that, I'd like to have your grandfather standing by the creek with that long rope of his. Then if it looks like we are going on downstream, he can throw us a line. Your Pap could lasso us if he had to."

Vern sat down heavily on the edge of the raft. He stared at the ground.

This was the first time the dangers of the voyage had been mentioned. Up until this moment, it had been all glory and excitement and fame, the stuff of which adventure stories are made.

"What if we don't land at all?" Vern said thoughtfully, his voice barely audible over the rush of the creek.

"That would mean," Michael said, "that we keep on going. Then if we still don't land, we'd go over White Water Falls." Michael swallowed before he continued. "White Water Falls—I saw a picture of it in the newspaper last week—White Water Falls right now looks exactly like Niagara Falls."

"The last thing I want to do is go over White Water Falls," Vern said.

"Take it from me, going over White Water Falls would be the last thing you would ever do."

There was a silence, then Vern said, "One time my brother Junior—" Vern only had one brother, but this was important enough to identify him. "One time my brother Junior was going over the falls, and he put blowed-up garbage bags under his arms and waded out in the creek. Then he got scared and didn't go."

"Your brother Junior's smarter than I thought he was."

"And that was before the flood."

"Maybe," Michael began. "No, never mind."

"Go on, say what you're thinking."

"Well, I was just thinking that we could tie a rope on the raft—like a tether, and test the current before we set out. Then if it doesn't feel just right, if it doesn't feel like we can stop anytime we want to, we can pull ourselves back to shore."

"That's a good idea."

Vern jumped to his feet. He was already pretty sure the current was not going to feel right. At least he was sure enough so that he didn't want to run up and call his family on the telephone.

Or maybe he should, he thought. Maybe he should al-

48

low Michael's mother to hear. It would be a sort of relief to hear her stern "Ab-so-lute-ly not!"

"Where are we going to get more rope though?" Michael said. "We've been using vines for the last hour."

"Clothesline?"

"We have a dryer."

"We could tear up some old sheets," Vern said.

"Whose?" Michael asked. "My mom gave us her one old sheet for the sail, remember?"

"All right then, more vine, but it's got to be strong vine, and we've got to braid it."

Both boys started up the hill. Both were relieved to be going into the woods for vines instead of starting down the creek. The creek at their backs seemed to have risen dramatically just since the interrupted countdown.

At the top of the hill, Vern paused. Michael looked at him.

"And if either one of us doesn't think we ought to go," Vern said, "then it's off. We won't go, right?"

Michael hesitated only one second before putting out his hand. Vern looked down in surprise. He had never shaken hands with anybody before; he thought only grown men shook hands. Obviously he had been wrong. This was a situation that clearly called for a handshake.

Vern took Michael's dirty hand in his and they shook.

The Electric Moment

PAP LEANED AGAINST A TREE. DROPS OF WATER dripped from the branches and rolled down his tired face, mingling with the sweat. Pap pulled out a ragged bandanna and mopped his brow.

"I got to rest, Mud," Pap said. He had begun to pant. "I ain't as young as I used to be." He stopped talking to save his breath. "Junior's going to have to wait on us just a little longer."

The truck horn had sounded one more time. Then it had stopped. Now there was only the rush of the creek and his own labored breathing.

Pap saw a nice boulder up the hill and he stumbled toward it. He sat down with a heavy sigh. His body sagged with fatigue.

"I knowed this rock was put here for a reason. Sometimes, Mud," he said, pausing again. "Sometimes it seems like the whole world's been made just for my comfort. I need a rock to set on, and one's right there. I need a tree to help me up a bank, there's a tree." There was another pause. Then, "A man can't ask more out of life than that."

Mud was using the rest time to move up and down the hill, nose to the ground. The only visible part of him was his tail, flying over the weeds.

Pap said, "Mud."

Dutifully Mud raised his head and looked in Pap's direction.

"I just wanted to know where you was. Go on about your business. Go on."

Mud disappeared into the weeds. Pap began to rub his arm.

Ever since Pap had started practicing his rope tricks—this was to be a surprise for the family—he was going to do his old rope routine on the rodeo circuit this summer if he could get in shape, but ever since he had started practicing, his arm had been hurting. Sometimes it hurt even when he hadn't practiced, like right now.

As usual, Pap shrugged off his pain. It would be worth it. What were a few aches and pains compared to being on the rodeo circuit again?

As Pap sat there on the stone, rubbing his arm, he remembered what a dashing figure he had been in those early days. He would come out in the arena dressed all in black—black hat, black boots with silver horse heads on the sides, black cowboy shirt, shiny black pants.

His ropes—he had different length ropes for different tricks—would be coiled beside him. One by one the announcer would call out the tricks. "Cowboy's Wedding Ring . . . Butterfly . . . Ocean Waves . . ."

Pap would twirl his ropes vertically, horizontally, step in and out of them, make them into curlicues. There wasn't anything he couldn't do with ropes when he was a young man.

His act came between events in those days, and so naturally he would not have been surprised if some of the people had left the stands—that was when people generally got refreshments and socialized, but they never left during his act.

They stayed in their seats, even the ladies. That's how he met his wife—Maida—she hung around to tell him how much she had enjoyed his act, and he took her picture with his Brownie Kodak.

His next-to-last trick was Around the World. He used a huge coil of rope, ninety feet long, for that. He made a loop and began to open it over his head, feeding out the rope so the loop got bigger and bigger.

When it was whizzing overhead, all ninety feet of it, when it reached full spread, Pap would give one final turn and let it drop around him like a skirt.

There was always extra interest in his last trick. It was Pap's specialty. As a closing stunt he wrote his name, one letter at a time, in the air with his rope.

"B!" The crowd spelled it out with the announcer, drowning him out. "L! O! S! S! O! M!"

Then Pap bowed and took off his black hat to the crowd. His hair was jet-black then too. The applause was like thunder.

The memory captured his mind for a moment. He could see himself in the arena, lit up so bright it was as if the sun itself had decided to ignore everybody in the universe and, for one glorious electric moment, spotlight him alone.

He blinked his eyes as the memory began to fade. "Of course," he went on, trying to bring himself down easy, "I probably couldn't spell my name anymore. I haven't got time to practice, but maybe I could get a silver cowboy shirt to match my hair. Maybe I could paint my old boots silver. Maybe I could—"

Mud bounded into sight then. He paused and looked at Pap for instructions. His tail wagged deep in the weeds, setting them in motion.

"Yes, we better be getting on home," Pap said. "We better go."

Still he continued to sit. He sighed. He closed his eyes for a moment. Then, rubbing his arm, he got up from the rock and started walking.

The Man on the Brindle Bull

MAGGIE WAS SITTING IN THE CONTESTANTS' GRAND-stand, eating a bucket of popcorn. She had never enjoyed anything so much in her life.

For the past two days, Maggie had had no appetite at all. "Now, you have to eat," her mom had told her. "You can't starve yourself and ride in rodeos."

"I'm not starving myself."

"You aren't getting sick, are you? I just don't know what I'm going to do if you get sick."

"No, Mom, I am not sick." Maggie shook off her hand. "I'm fine." Maggie didn't want her mother to know she couldn't eat because she was nervous.

"Well, then, why aren't you eating? This is one of the best foot-long hot dogs I've ever had. Is there something wrong with yours?"

"No."

"Then eat!"

"That's what I'm trying to do. Anyway, you're supposed to chew hot dogs a lot. People have choked to death on hot dogs."

"You don't have to tell me," her mother said, diverted at last. "My first cousin choked on one and almost died. That was before this new method that's running around. We pounded them on the back then."

"Did it work?"

"You know her—Maureen."

Maggie had nibbled at her hot dog, playing for time. Sooner or later her mom would see some of her friends and say, "Shug, do you mind if we drop you at the motel and go for a few beers?"

"Not at all," Maggie would answer. That would give her a chance to wrap up her hot dog and feed it later to a stray cat that hung around the motel.

Her mom had carried on so much about Maggie starving herself that Maggie thought she would be the happiest woman in the world when she started eating.

Well, now she was eating. She was wolfing down popcorn as fast as she could, and her mom didn't even notice. Her mom was sitting beside Maggie, twisting her neckerchief between her fingers. Maggie couldn't understand why her mom was nervous. The performance was over. They had done great.

Again she offered her mom some popcorn. Her mom didn't notice. "Mom, popcorn?" Vicki Blossom glanced down at the bucket as if she were trying to figure out what it was. Then she shook her head.

Maggie didn't understand that either. Her mom loved popcorn. Her mom always said rodeo popcorn was her favorite food in the world.

Maggie heard a vendor yell, "Ice cream." She ate even faster. As soon as she finished this bucket she was going to get a Popsicle. Rodeo Popsicles were good too.

Maggie shoved her white hat up on her head. The late-afternoon sun had dropped behind the stands and was no longer shining in her eyes, but Maggie didn't want to take off her hat. It identified her as one of the Wrangler Riders.

The rodeo was almost over. Only the bull riding event and the bull fighting were left.

Joe Nevada was saying, "While we're setting up the fence for the bull riding event, which only takes two or three minutes, we'll say a word about the bull riding contest. The tough contest is reflected by the scoreboard. We had nearly eighty contestants this year."

Maggie was eating popcorn out of the palm of her hand now.

"Now, here's the first bull rider, folks, out of chute eight. Boy, talk about breaking out of there. I like this. We got one going. Look, Ma, there's nothing to it. Riding bulls on a Sunday afternoon. You don't even get your chaps dirty. It's a seventy-eight score for Steve."

Maggie turned up her bucket and let the last crumbs of popcorn fall into her mouth. She glanced around. A sunburned girl with a cooler was right in front of the stand. "Ice cream!" she called.

Maggie wiped the grease off her mouth with the back of her hand. "Over here," she called. To her mom she said, "Can I please have fifty cents? I'm starving."

Her mother didn't answer.

Maggie held out her hand. She snapped her fingers to get her mom's attention.

Her mom said, "Not right now," in a tense way.

"Mom—"

"Don't bother me."

Maggie looked hard at her mom. She was startled by the expression on her mother's face.

"What's wrong?"

"Nothing."

"I know something's wrong. Mom, maybe you shouldn't be watching this. Maybe we should leave. You don't have to watch it just because you said you could. If it brings back what happened to Daddy . . ."

"I want to watch it, all right? Oh, what do you need?"

"Nothing, never mind."

"What do you need?"

"Fifty cents," Maggie said.

"Here, now don't bother me again." Vicki Blossom reached in her jeans pocket and handed Maggie a crumpled five-dollar bill.

Maggie didn't want the Popsicle anymore but she bought it, pulled off the paper, and took a bite. She offered it to her mother. As she had figured, her mother didn't even notice.

"Why don't we go back to the motel?" Maggie said. "Please, Mom."

Her mom didn't hear her.

"And now in chute four we have the match of the year," the announcer said. "A two-thousand-pound brindle bull, voted Bucking Bull of the Year, and he's being ridden by one of the all-time greats—Cody Gray."

Maggie's eyes were riveted on her mom now. Vicki Blossom was holding her neckerchief over her mouth.

With a sickening lunge of her stomach, Maggie remembered that was what her mom used to do when she watched Cotton Blossom ride.

Her mom's eyes were fixed on chute four. Maggie had

never seen her mom so intent before. It was as if Maggie's father were in chute four, instead of some stranger.

"Is it somebody you know?" Maggie asked.

Her Popsicle was forgotten. The ice cream was melting, running down her fingers.

"A friend."

"I never heard of him before."

"I asked you not to bother me."

"I want to know."

"Oh, Maggie, you've heard of Cody Gray all your life."

"No, I haven't. Who is he?"

Her mother didn't answer.

"When did he get to be a friend?"

Again, no answer.

Her mom reached out abruptly and took Maggie's arm. She squeezed it tight. This was something else Maggie remembered from the old days. "Let me hold on to you," her mom was always saying when Cotton rode bulls.

The announcer said, "This bull has only been ridden two times in two and a half years, so you may be seeing rodeo history here this afternoon. Here they come!"

Vicki Blossom put her neckerchief over her eyes. Maggie was astonished. Her mom had never had to hide her eyes before, not even when her dad rode. She watched her mother intently and then turned with equal intensity to the man who had just come out on the brindle bull.

"Look's like a good-un," the announcer said. "No, looks like a great one! Yessir, this is rodeo history—a hundred-and-fifty-pound man mastering a two-thousand-pound bull. Cody won National Champion last year in Las Vegas, and it looks like he's going to be a champion today."

Maggie said, "It's over, Mom."

58

Vicki Blossom dropped her neckerchief into her lap. Without the neckerchief, her face looked unprotected.

The announcer said, "Let's watch the scoreboard—there it is, folks. Ninety! You have seen rodeo history this afternoon right here in—"

Maggie didn't hear the rest. Her mom was on her feet, beaming. She was clapping so hard it must have stung her hands.

Maggie let her Popsicle drop down between the floor-boards. It plopped unnoticed onto the dust below.

Then, with a sigh, she began to wipe the ice cream that had melted down her fingers onto her Wrangler jeans.

Letting Go

"DON'T LET GO!"

"I won't. Don't you let go!"

These were terse commands yelled loudly, although Michael and Vern were only ten inches apart.

Then: "Watch it!"

"I am. You watch it!"

"I am!"

Michael and Vern had looped vines around two small trees on shore. They had gradually let the raft and themselves out into the creek. At present they were exactly six inches from land.

It seemed a lot farther to the boys. The water swept around the raft, giving the impression that they were in midstream. The way the current pulled at the raft gave both of them new respect for currents.

Both boys were in a crouch like surfers in the curl of a wave. Neither boy felt secure enough to stand erect, and they kept glancing uneasily over their shoulders. The creek at their backs now looked as wide as the Mississippi River.

"This was a rotten idea," Michael said in a strained voice. His vines were twisted so tightly in his fingers that the circulation was being cut off.

"You didn't think so this morning."

"That was this morning."

"And now?" Vern's voice was strained too.

"How many times do I have to say it? This was a rotten idea."

"All right, if you think it's such a rotten idea, all you have to say is that you want to quit."

Vern looked at Michael.

Michael hesitated. "I'm not a quitter," he said.

"I didn't say you were a quitter, but if you do want to quit, now's the time to say so."

"Do you want to?" Michael asked.

"If you do."

"No, you have to say it."

Vern's vines were beginning to fray. The outside bark had rubbed off on the tree, and the green inside was showing. The circulation in his fingers was cut off too. He didn't have any feeling in his fingertips.

"I'm ready to quit," he said.

"Me too," said Michael. "Let's pull back to shore."

"But pull gently. We don't want too much pressure on these vines. Mine are starting to fray."

"Mine too."

"Are you pulling?"

"Yes, are you?"

"Yes."

"Then why aren't we moving?"

"I don't know."

"It's the current!"

61

"I know. Just don't let go."

"I won't. Don't you let go."

Vern tried to get a better grip on his vines. One strand snapped. The sound was as loud in Vern's ears as gunfire, and just as frightening.

Vern edged closer to the side of the raft. His toes curled over the log's edge. He judged the distance.

"Maybe we better jump for it," he gasped.

"And lose the raft?"

"Yes."

"I'll count so we go at the same time. Don't jump till I do, all right?"

Michael nodded.

Vern said, "One—two—three—"

Vern did not get to say the word "Go." On the count of three, the last of Vern's vines snapped. Vern fell back onto the raft. The raft swung out into the creek. Michael, set to jump, was slung sideways. He fell too.

The raft rocked dangerously in the water as the boys scrambled to their knees. They both had one thing in mind—jumping for shore.

Jumping was impossible. They were already in midstream.

Michael and Vern looked at each other in horror. Then they glanced down at the cold, muddy water lapping at their knees. The sail flapped wildly over their heads.

"How good a swimmer are you?" Vern gasped.

"Not that good," Michael answered.

With sinking hearts, they watched the familiar part of the shore pass from view—the white roof of Michael's house, the weather vane on the barn, the pecan trees.

"Then paddle!" Vern said.

"We lost the paddles when we fell!"

"Use your hands!"

In a crouch they began to pull their hands through the water.

"This won't work. Break off some deck! Quick!"

"Good idea! Deck!"

Vern pulled on a board. It snapped off easily. Michael's did too. They began to sweep the boards through the water, aiming for the closest bank.

"I think it's working. Paddle hard."

"I am! You paddle hard."

The raft moved around the bend, got caught in an eddy and turned sideways.

"Paddle on the other side!"

"Right."

The boys were so intent on paddling that they did not look up and see the bridge.

The bridge was a wooden one that led to the Houston farm. Normally it was twelve feet higher than the level of the creek. Now it was at the exact height of Michael and Vern's heads.

The raft was on a stretch of straight water. It picked up speed. The boys were bent over, paddling. Vern was yelling, "It's working!" when they hit the bridge.

They struck with such force that both boys were thrown forward. Their faces plunged into the creek. They inhaled water and came up choking for air.

They were hanging off the back of the raft. They pulled themselves back and clung, gagging and coughing, to the slick boards.

"The bridge," Vern gasped. "We hit the bridge."

"My head," Michael moaned.

"Mine too." Vern didn't dare let go to feel the damage. "Can you paddle?"

"I don't think so."

"We'll be at my house before long," Vern gasped. "Can you yell?"

Yelling was the one thing that appealed to Vern. He had wanted to do it the moment the voyage began.

"Yes," Michael said.

"We better start now."

They threw back their heads and screamed at the top of their lungs.

"Helllllp!"

"Helllllp!"

"Helllllp!"

Junior's Dump

JUNIOR SQUINTED INTO THE DARK CRAWL SPACE. HE HAD called Dump five times, and Dump still had not come.

Junior didn't like to go under the house. It was too dark, too scary, and it smelled funny. He was not going to go one inch farther than he absolutely had to.

"Where are you, Dump?" he called.

He heard the sound of Dump's tail brushing against the ground.

"I hear you but I don't see you," Junior said.

He pushed aside his paper bag.

"Nothing works for me today," Junior grumbled, getting ready to start crawling. "Pap won't come when I call him. Now you won't either, Dump."

Junior wiggled forward, pulling himself along with his elbows.

"Well, I can't do anything about Pap, but I can do something about you. I'm going to make you come, Dump."

At last Junior had something purposeful to do. "You're coming with me, frogs or no frogs."

He stopped crawling when he mentioned frogs and

looked down. He didn't want to mash one. He didn't want one jumping up in his face.

He peered into the darkness. A lot of bushes grew around the house—and these bushes were seventy years old, so they were big and thick. No sunlight came through. No fresh air got in either.

"I should have brought matches," Junior said.

He propped his head in his hands to let his eyes get used to the darkness. He didn't want to move until he could see exactly what was ahead of him.

As his eyes adjusted, he caught sight of Dump. Even in the dark Dump was easy to see because he was white with brown spots. "He's just like a Dalmatian," was the way Junior described his dog to other people, "only his spots are brown and his hair's long."

"Dump! I see you! Get over here!"

Dump wagged his tail, sweeping some dried leaves back and forth in the loose dirt.

"Didn't you hear me calling you? Come on."

Dump hesitated.

"Come on, Dump, nice Dump. Good dog."

Pap had told Junior he had to speak nicely to Dump because Dump had had a hard life. "This dog," Pap had said, stroking him gently on his lap, "this dog's been kicked, he's been hit, he's been starved, and he's been thrown into a garbage dumpster to die. Now, every time you call this dog, Junior, and he don't come, you remember what he's been through. He'll get to trust you, but it's going to take time."

"I'm not going to hurt you, Dump, I just want you to go somewhere with me."

Junior pulled himself forward on his elbows.

Dump's tail stopped wagging.

"I said I wasn't going to do anything to you," Junior said. "Have I ever hurt you? No. Have I ever hit you? No. Even if you did something wrong, even if you bit me, Dump, would I hit you? No. You might not believe this, but I have never, ever hit one single person or one single animal in my entire life."

Dump gave a feeble wag of his tail.

"That's better. Now, remember this. I'm not going to hurt you. I like you. Actually, I love—"

Junior stopped. A strange, musty scent hung in the still air. Junior had smelled this only once before, but he had never forgotten it.

He had been in the garden with Pap, weeding, when Pap had stopped. He had lifted his head, leaning slightly on the handle of the hoe. It was a hot morning; there wasn't enough of a breeze to rustle the corn stalks.

"Smell that?" Pap said.

At first Junior could smell only the newly turned earth, and so he took in a deeper breath. There it was—a sweet, musty smell, the smell of old, dark bread.

"What is it, Pap?"

"Snake," Pap said.

Junior scrambled to his feet.

"Anytime you smell that, Junior, you know a snake's nearby."

Now here it was again. The same sweet musty smell. Junior was smelling it for the second time in his life, and a chill went up his spine.

His eyes darted around the dim crawl space. He didn't see the snake, but he knew it was there. Nothing else smelled like that.

"Come on, Dump, come on! We got to get out of here."

The urgency in his voice made Dump's tail stop wagging.

"Come on, will you? Come on?"

Junior reached out to beckon. Dump took one step backward. And in that unguarded moment the snake struck.

Dump screamed with pain. Junior didn't even know dogs could make sounds like that. Junior screamed too.

Dump leapt into the air, striking his head on the floorboards of the house. He twisted in agony and then he rushed past Junior so fast Junior didn't have a chance to grab him.

Dump's sharp yelps of pain grew fainter as Dump ran into the woods. Junior peered into the shadows. There it was, the snake. It blended in perfectly with the dirt, the dead leaves, the old wood. It was not a black snake.

In the cabbages that day, leaning on his hoe, Pap had told Junior about snakes. "They can't hear, but they feel vibrations, Junior. That snake knows you and me are standing here in the cabbages."

Junior knew that at the moment his whole body was vibrating so hard every snake in the county knew his exact location.

The snake slithered around the chimney and out of sight. Junior backed out of the crawl space fast. He scrambled to his feet and ran down the hill to the creek.

When he got to the bank, he started screaming, "Pap, Pap, Dump's been snake-bit. Pap, Oh, Pap!"

"I'll see you back at the stables," Vicki Blossom said to Maggie.

68

Maggie had been pretending to watch the bull fighting, but actually she had been watching her mother out of the sides of her eyes.

"Where are you going, Mom? I want to go with you. I'm tired of watching this."

"I just want to congratulate a friend, Maggie. I'll see you later."

"Why can't I come?"

"Maggie, we aren't Siamese twins. We can be apart for five minutes, can't we?"

"Cody Gray?" Maggie asked. "Is that who you're going to congratulate?"

"Yes! You got any objections?"

Maggie didn't answer, and her mom didn't wait for one.

Things were beginning to click together in Maggie's mind. Ever since they got to Tucson, her mother had been going out at night. "With the girls," she said, but every night she had come home late. Maggie wasn't sure of the exact time, but every morning it was harder and harder to get her mother up.

And her mom had started dressing up a lot for these nights with the girls. She'd even started painting her eyelids to match her outfits.

Maggie sat alone, going over these things in her mind. The bull fighting had started, but Maggie wasn't paying attention.

In the arena, the bull ignored the fighter and ran after one of the clowns. The clown ran for a barrel and dove inside.

Joe Nevada laughed. "That's the fastest that clown ever ran. I had a dog used to run like that before we cured him of worms."

The crowd laughed. Maggie didn't.

Maggie was suddenly tired. The sun . . . the noise . . . the dust. She wished she hadn't eaten so much popcorn.

"Excuse me," Maggie said. She crawled over the knees of the woman beside her. The woman took Maggie's arm to steady her.

The woman said, "I can't believe you're leaving during the bull fighting. This is the best event."

"I ate too much popcorn," Maggie said.

"You kids never learn."

"Oh, I wouldn't say never. Sometimes we do," Maggie answered.

She hurried around the stands, her hat low on her head. She passed the pens where the bulls, horses, and calves stood, quiet now. There were yells from the crowd as the bull fighter made a close pass.

Maggie stopped. She slipped behind a horse trailer. Her mother was just ahead, joining a group of people in bright shirts, well-worn hats.

Maggie's eyes narrowed with concentration. She bit her bottom lip. She worked her hands into the pockets of her jeans.

The crowd shifted to make room for Vicki Blossom. It was as if they had shifted like this before, as if they all knew Vicki Blossom belonged inside the circle. Vicki Blossom moved quickly. Before the crowd closed around her, Maggie saw her throw her arms around Cody.

"Cody, love," she cried. "Oh, shug, you were wonderful!" And then, as Maggie pulled back into the shadows, her mother kissed him.

71

The Rope Trick of the Year

"Whoa, slow down, Junior, slow down," Pap said. "Take it easy."

Junior had run down the hill and into Pap's arms so fast he had spun Pap all the way around.

"Now, what's all the yelling about? Start at the beginning."

Junior regained his balance. He caught his breath. Then he began shifting anxiously from foot to foot.

"The beginning," Pap said again.

"That is the beginning, Pap! Dump's been bit by a snake. *A snake!*" Junior used two big gestures with the last two words, the way he would if he'd been saying them on a stage.

"Now, calm down. What kind of snake was it?"

"I don't know."

"Junior, I've taught you about snakes. Did it have markings on it?"

"I think so. Anyway it wasn't a black snake."

Junior tried to turn Pap around and head him in the

72

right direction like somebody starting a game of blind man's bluff. Pap rocked back on his heels.

"We got to find him, Pap, and give him some medicine."

Junior gave up on pushing Pap. He grabbed Pap's hand and began tugging him toward home.

"Junior, hold on. There ain't no medicine you can give a dog for a snake bite."

"I know there is. There has to be."

"A snake-bit dog either gets well on his own or he don't."

Junior turned his face up to Pap.

"My best dog when I was a boy got bit by a water moccasin on the nose."

"The black hunting dog?" Junior asked.

"The pit bull—Buster, we called him. Buster got bit right there." Pap pinched his left nostril. "Buster went running off just like you claim Dump did and didn't come back for four days."

"Four days!"

"That's right. Buster was an ugly-looking dog anyway, but when he came home after those four days, he was the ugliest thing you ever saw outside the moving pictures. They had an Ugly Dog Contest that year at the fair, and didn't no other dog stand a chance. Buster took the blue ribbon and the red ribbon. The yellow ribbon went to a little Mexican dog that didn't have no hair."

"And he lived?"

"To a ripe old age," Pap said.

"I think Dump got bit on the leg."

"Well, that helps his odds. If you got to get bit, an extremity is the best place."

"A hind leg is an extremity?"

"Yes."

Junior sighed. "It was sort of my fault, Pap. I was crawling under the house and Dump was afraid I was coming to do something to him, and so he stepped back to get away from me and—"

Suddenly Pap said, "Hush!" He threw up his head. He cupped one hand behind his ear so he could hear better.

Junior started to finish the story about Dump, but Pap grabbed his arm and squeezed it hard. He said again, "Hush, Junior!"

"What is it, Pap?"

"Lord, somebody else is in trouble. Hear that? They're yelling for help. It sounds like Vern."

Pap started up the creek. He went from tree to tree, pulling himself along. Junior followed.

"It is Vern!" Pap said.

He moved up the hill toward the barn. Now that there were no trees to help him along, Pap was making swimming motions with his arms.

He had to get to the top of the hill. He would have a good view from there. And he didn't have any time to waste.

"Vern needs my help," he reminded himself as he ran. "Vern needs me."

Beside him Junior was running sideways. "What are you going to do, Pap?"

"Help Vern," Pap gasped.

The cries were getting louder. Pap knew now that they were coming from the creek. At the crest of the hill, he paused, with one hand over his heart, one hand shielding his eyes from the afternoon sun.

He saw nothing. He turned and ran for the barn. He

knew that if Vern was out in the middle of the creek, he might need to be pulled in. Pap wanted a rope in his hand.

Pap's ropes were coiled in loops in a wooden box just inside the barn door. No one ever bothered Pap's ropes, so they were always where Pap could get them. Even when Junior or Vern desperately needed rope, as they often did, they never took Pap's.

Pap rushed into the barn. Birds flew out, startled from their perches. Pap never saw them.

He grabbed his longest rope, the ninety-foot one he used for "Around the World." With the rope in one hand, Pap ran toward the swollen creek.

With his other hand, he clutched his heart, trying to keep it from jumping out of his chest.

He stood on the bank, heart thudding unevenly like an old overworked machine. He ignored the pain as he uncoiled his rope.

"Pap—"

"Out of my way, Junior."

With one deft shake of his hand, the noose twirled at Pap's side. The rope turned easily, but the rest of Pap's body was tight, tense. His chin jutted out stiffly in his old sagging face.

"It's two voices," Junior said, listening. "Michael must be with Vern. They must have fallen into the creek together. You'll have to rope both of them, Pap."

"Oh, Lord, here they are," Pap gasped. He had been waiting for it, but still it was a shock.

The raft swept around the bend, obviously at the mercy of the strong current. It was low in the water now. The boys were at the back, desperately kicking, trying to push the raft toward the shore.

75

"Get ready, Pap," Junior said.

Pap didn't answer. He said "Lord, help me" as the raft hit a ripple in the current. The front tipped up, and the back dipped even lower in the water.

"Hold on!" Pap yelled. Under his breath he said, "They're going to drown before they get to me."

"Just don't miss," Junior advised.

Pap waded into the muddy water. At his side, the rope twirled evenly, effortlessly. Junior ran up the creek toward the raft, beckoning it to shore.

"Over this way," he shouted. "Over here."

Pap waded deeper into the water. He would have his best shot at roping the boys when they got to the bend in the creek. The loop of rope was twirling at shoulder height now so it wouldn't touch the water.

All week long, while the creek had been rising, Pap had been watching it from a rocking chair on the porch. Pap knew that the raft would probably spin around at least once before sweeping around the turn. Pap had watched logs and trash get caught there in an eddy all week.

He got set. He edged farther out into the creek. The muddy water filled his high-topped shoes, splashed on his swollen knees. He took another step. The water rushed around his thighs.

"I'll get you at the fishing hole," he called to the boys.

He didn't know whether they could hear him or not. Both of them were yelling their heads off.

"The fishing hole!" Pap pointed to the inner curve of the creek where he and Vern had fished so often. "Get ready!"

Vern nodded. He freed one hand and waved it to show he heard. He was ready.

76

Pap wound the rope around his head. The loop grew bigger. The rope was whizzing now, a long powerful curl of rope.

"Help me, Lord," Pap said.

At the exact moment that the raft paused in the bend of the creek, caught in the current, Pap let the rope out across the water in a long graceful arc.

It was a perfect throw. The boys watched it come. It was the most beautiful thing Junior had ever seen in his life, an absolutely perfect throw. Both Vern and Michael put up a hand, and both of them caught the rope at the same time.

"You got them! You did it! You got them!" Junior cried. He was dancing with pleasure. "You did it, Pap!"

And then, in that moment of triumph, a terrible thing happened. Pap let go of his end of the rope. He clutched his chest with both hands and stumbled up the bank.

Junior cried, "Pap!"

Junior was too stunned to move.

"Pap!"

Pap didn't answer. He grabbed a tree for support. He leaned there for a long moment. His body was suddenly stiff, bowed backward in an arch.

And then Pap let go. His body twisted around the trunk of the tree like an old vine. Then he lay over the roots and didn't move.

Junior didn't move either.

Behind him the raft swept around the bend and out of sight, with Pap's rope trailing uselessly behind.

The Fourth Postcard

MAGGIE WAS IN ROOM 104 OF THE BAR NONE MOTEL. She was alone, sitting at the desk. For thirty minutes she had been trying to write four postcards.

She had gotten these postcards when she and her mom first checked into the motel, but she had waited to write them until after the rodeo. That way she could tell everybody how good the Wrangler Riders had been.

"I know how you'll start them," her mom had said, teasing her. "Today was the best day of my life. I was wonderful!"

"Oh, Mom," Maggie had said, but she did like the first part. "Today was the best day of my life."

The four cards were lined in front of her on the desk. All were glorified views of the Bar None Motel. The blue pool looked Olympic size. The tables around it had umbrellas. There were enough flowers to open a nursery.

Maggie had started all four of her cards, but not the way she had planned. This had been the best day of her life, but it had also been the worst. Therefore, all she had written so far were Dear Vern, Dear Pap, Dear Junior, and Dear Ralphie.

"You won't mind eating by yourself, will you, shug," her mother had said. She had been in the bathroom, at the mirror, painting her eyelids green. "You can run right across the street to Bojangle's or next door to the Bar-B-Q Barn. You still have some money left from that five I gave you this afternoon, don't you?"

"Yes, but why can't we have supper together?"

"I promised the girls I'd eat with them."

"The girls?"

"The girls and whoever else wants to join us, I guess. Maggie, you know how rodeo people like to get together." She poked her head out of the bathroom to give Maggie a disappointed look. One eyelid was green, the other plain. "I never thought you would want me to miss a good time."

"Mom, we could have a good time together. We could go to a movie."

Her mom stepped back into the bathroom. When she was out of sight she called, "It's already settled. Cody Gray's picking me up." She stepped into Maggie's view with both eyelids green.

A horn honked twice outside the door. "There he is." She hesitated, then said, "Maggie, come on out, and congratulate him."

"I don't want to."

"Please, shug, I want you two to get to know each other."

"No, Mom."

"You sure have gotten hard to get along with." She gave

Maggie a disappointed look, and then she opened the motel door and broke into a smile.

Maggie crossed quickly to the window. She yanked aside the drape to watch her mother getting into the silver convertible.

In one motion, Vicki Blossom opened the car door, slid in, and hugged Cody Gray so hard she knocked his hat off his head. Maggie couldn't hear what Cody said because the motel air conditioner clicked on at that exact moment, but it made them both laugh.

Her mother looked up then, still laughing, and pointed to Maggie in the window. She waved. Maggie whipped the drapes shut.

Ever since they'd driven off, Maggie had been trying to write postcards. Once again she shifted them around on the desk. This time Ralphie's ended up in front of her. That was good. She needed Ralphie's special magic tonight.

Ralphie was her best friend. Ralphie could—he had proved this again and again—do anything. His specialty, he'd once said, was the impossible. She would have given anything in the world to have Ralphie walk in the motel door.

I wonder if I could call him, she thought. I wouldn't say anything about my mom, I'd just—

With a sigh she began to write.

I wish you could have been at the rodeo. You're good luck. I never fall when you're watching. Well, I didn't fall today, but I did have a little bad luck. Mom says I can stay next week too, but I may come on home on the bus.

She hesitated, vaguely dissatisfied with what she had written. She wanted to do it over. The trouble was, she had already written the names on the other cards. Well, it would have to do.

She read the message again. Then she thought about whether she should sign it "Love, Maggie" or "Your friend, Maggie." Finally she figured out that if she added one more line, the postcard would be full and she wouldn't have to commit herself.

"See you soon," she wrote, "Maggie Blossom." Now, for some reason, she was even more dissatisfied. Maybe I could squeeze the word "love" in right there, she thought. She did squeeze it in, but now the card was ruined. The word "love" stood out. She had written it small, but for some reason it had turned out to be the biggest word on the whole card.

She looked at the remaining cards, and then she did what she had felt like doing from the first, swept them all into the trashcan. She threw down her pen. She put her head in her hands.

Maggie was more unsettled than she had ever been in her life. Maggie hated her mother.

For a long time Maggie had never understood how anybody could dislike their parents. She had thought kids at school who claimed they did were just exaggerating. She could never hate her mother. Her mother was like a wonderful older sister.

Maggie lifted her head. Her eyes were slits in her sunburned face.

"She ruined everything," she said aloud. "This could have been the best day of my entire life, and she ruined it!"

81

She got up abruptly and began to pace.

"Why did she have to ruin everything?" she asked again. "She's disgusting. She really makes me sick."

Maggie walked around the bed.

"And Cody Gray is disgusting too in that stupid big-time Cadillac!"

She came to the wall and stopped. She had never noticed before how small this motel room was. And there was nothing to do. You could write postcards or go out and swim in the scummy pool with a lot of drunk cowboys. That was it.

You could watch TV. She walked to the set and jabbed the On button.

The wheel of fortune was spinning. "Disgusting," Maggie said. "Greedy, disgusting people!"

She began walking around the motel room like an animal in a zoo cage—around the bed to the bathroom, back around the bed to the desk, around the bed to the bathroom . . .

She was going around the bed for the fourteenth time when the phone rang.

By Snake Creek's Rushing Waters

"PAP! PAP! WAKE UP!"

Junior was on his knees beside Pap. He was shivering. His hands were tucked under his arms.

"Pap! Talk to me. Tell me what to do. Pap, wake up! Please!"

Pap had not moved a muscle since he fell. Junior had known when Pap wilted around the tree in that terrible way that Pap was in trouble, so much trouble that for a long time Junior had not been able to move either.

It had taken him five long minutes to get up the courage to go to Pap. He still had not touched him.

Slowly he stretched out one trembling hand. He tugged Pap's sleeve.

"Pap?"

There was no answer. Junior took a pinch of Pap's shirt and shook the cloth. "Are you all right?"

No answer.

Junior twisted his fingers into Pap's overall straps. He shook the straps. They moved back and forth on Pap's solid back.

"What can I do to help? What can I do? Listen to me, Pap. I'll do anything you want me to do. Just tell me."

When Pap still didn't answer, Junior started to cry.

"You want me to go for help or what? I don't know what to do."

He shook the overall straps harder.

"Answer me!"

Junior yanked the straps as hard as if he were pulling reins. Pap came away from the tree trunk then. He rolled over onto his back. His arm fell loosely across Junior's knees. His mouth fell open. He unseeing eyes looked up at Junior's face.

Junior screamed. He covered his face with both hands. Blindly, he stumbled to his feet.

Hands over his eyes, he backed away. He lifted his hands and peeked under his fingers to see where he was. The ground looked unfamiliar, farther away than it should have been.

He felt so strange that he put his hands on his head. His head felt light, as if it were rising, as if it weren't attached to his body anymore. Maybe that was why the ground was so far away. His head was rising like a balloon.

"Somebody, please help me," he mumbled. "Somebody, please help me."

His legs kept carrying him backward over the distant ground until he felt the chilling waters of Snake Creek on his bare ankles. He looked down in surprise.

He wept into his trembling hands.

"Something terrible's happened to Pap and Vern's gone and I'm all by myself and I don't know what to do. I don't know what to do. I just don't know what to do."

He turned from side to side, wagging his head in a

hopeless animal movement, beating on his forehead with his fists, trying to make his brain give him an answer.

He could hardly breathe at all now.

"What am I going to do," he moaned, "oh, what am I going to do?"

He threw back his head, opened his eyes, and looked at the blinding blue sky. He was now gasping for breath. Each breath seemed his last. One more breath, and he would stumble up the hill, like Pap, and fall lifeless around the nearest tree.

The prospect was so real and so terrifying that Junior screamed.

He started to run. He ran up the hill, blindly, his arms flailing in the air. At the top of the hill, he stopped. He twisted from one side to the other. His eyes were wild.

Nothing looked familiar—not the house he had lived in all his life, not the barn, the trees.

He swirled around. Suddenly danger was everywhere, hiding, waiting to jump out. If you looked away for a second—like if you looked at your brother, then danger would strike your grandfather. If you looked away again, it might get you.

Junior heard a new noise, a shout. It was his own name, but Junior didn't even recognize that.

He turned. He felt dizzy. He put his hands to his head again, holding it in place. His eyes flickered wildly over the creek, the path, the sky.

And then, at last, Junior saw something he knew, one familiar thing. It was the most beautiful sight of Junior's life.

There, coming over the hill, swinging her crook—and

with the sun behind her, shining like something off a Sunday school paper—was Mad Mary.

She was hurrying toward him, holding out her arms.

"Junior!" she cried again.

Mary's ragged sleeves waved a welcome, and with a strangled cry Junior ran toward them.

The Snake Creek Crash

"Tree! There's a tree!" Michael screamed as they swept around a bend in the creek.

Ever since that terrible moment when they had caught the rope, thinking they were safe, and then watched Pap stumble up the creek bank and collapse, Michael and Vern had been silent. They had been in a state of shock.

Anyway, there had been no hope of anyone hearing their cries for help. The fields they passed were empty. There were no houses. It was a struggle now just to keep their heads above water.

The boards they had nailed down with such care had come loose. Most of the upper deck had been swept away. The mast had snapped off when they hit the bridge. They were now clinging to the logs. Neither of the boys thought of these logs as the Queen. The Queen was dead.

Vern's head snapped up when Michael yelled, "Tree!" He whipped his hair from his eyes.

Ahead, a large oak tree lay across the creek. It was an old tree, its trunk was three feet thick. The high water had eroded the soil around its rotting roots, and that morning the oak had ended its ninety years of life by toppling across the muddy water.

At first the sight of the tree filled Vern with dread. It was like the bridge, only they would not be able to duck under.

Then he heard Michael yell, "Grab it!"

Michael and Vern began kicking their feet, aiming for the trunk of the tree. Their hands were out, palms up, like beggars.

When their fingers touched the first leaves, they grabbed so hard, so desperately, the water was whipped into foam. Twigs snapped. Leaves tore off in their hands.

"I got one," Vern cried finally as his fingers curled around the first solid limb he had found. He was deep in the tree now. He couldn't even see Michael. He began to pull himself, hand over hand, along the limb toward the shore.

There was a scary moment as he felt the logs sweep out from under him, another scary moment when his body kept floating with the current. For a moment he was on his back, looking up into the branches.

Then, deep in the leaves he saw a branch large enough to bear his weight. He scissor-kicked hard. He reached up. His hand grasped the wood. Then, wrapping his legs around the branch, he pulled himself out of the water. The limb sagged a little beneath his weight, but he knew he was safe.

"Michael, did you make it?" He waited with his heart in his throat for the answer.

"I'm here."

"Pull yourself over where I am."

"I can't see you."

"I'm on a limb."

Michael's head came into view below. "I see you," Vern cried. "Come on up. I'll move over and make room."

"I can't reach that high."

"Well, wait, let me stand up and I'll bend the limb down to you."

Vern got to his feet. His knees were trembling. Carefully he put his weight on the limb.

"Can you get it?"

Michael grabbed the limb. Vern bent and clutched him under the arm. Slowly, with Michael climbing and Vern pulling, Michael got out of the stream.

Vern scooted aside to make room. The boys rested for a moment, hearts pumping hard, chests heaving, heads throbbing, while the creek raged beneath them.

Finally Michael said, "We made it." Then in a louder voice, "We made it!"

"I know."

"We made it!"

"I know."

He threw back his head. "We made it!"

Vern said, "You ready to climb to shore?"

"Yes."

"Follow me."

"You don't seem to realize. Vern, we made it!"

"I realize." He began crawling, hand over hand, up the trunk of the tree. "You coming, Michael?"

"I'm right behind you."

Vern reached the thickest part of the trunk, and he got to his feet and walked the rest of the way. He jumped onto the wet ground and fell forward onto his knees.

He was in a stubble field, but even the stubbles felt

good. Michael dropped beside him, and then both boys lay down, embracing the earth.

"We made it," Michael said again. He felt the back of his head with one hand. "I've got a knock right there," he said. "Do you?"

Vern didn't check. He said, "I've got to get home." As he spoke the words, his teeth chattered.

"Oh, sure," Michael answered. "I'm sorry. For a minute I forgot about your grandfather."

"I know."

Vern got to his feet. His clothes were plastered to his body. His hair stuck to his face. He was shivering.

Michael scrambled to his feet too. "What do you think happened to him?" he asked. Vern looked so pitiful that Michael began to pull at his own clothes, to squeeze out the water, to run his hands over his hair, to make himself presentable.

"I don't know."

"Did he ever fall like that before?"

"No."

"Maybe he fainted. My grandmother fainted in church one time. It was during a hymn."

"Maybe it was a faint." Vern began walking. He wrapped his arms around his body to control the shivering. "But I don't think so."

Mad Mary and Junior

"YOU HAVE GOT TO LET GO OF ME, JUNIOR," MAD MARY said.

"I can't!" Junior sobbed into her ragged clothes.

"Junior!"

"I can't, I just can't!"

She pushed him back so he had to look at her. He closed his eyes and shook his head blindly back and forth. He held her clothes so tightly that the old cloth ripped in his hands as he swayed.

"Junior, I have got to see to your grandfather. Now, you can either come with me or go up to the house. But let go!"

Junior did not answer so she said, "I mean it, Junior! We're wasting time."

Junior thought about it. "I'll go with you." His voice wavered. "But I can't look."

"That's better. Junior, I got to make sure whether he's dead or passed out."

"I think he's dead."

"Well, don't be too sure. I found a possum one time,

took him home, got ready to skin him, and he blinked. I said, 'Well, that blink just saved your life.'"

Junior stumbled down the hill, his face buried again in her clothes. He heard her say, "Shoo!" then, "Git!" and he knew they were passing Mud. Then they stopped, and Junior knew they were beside his grandfather.

Mad Mary knelt. Junior pulled her skirt tighter across his eyes.

"He's not dead," she said.

"What? What? How do you know?"

"His heart's beating. You could have found that out, Junior, if you'd bothered to put your hand down his shirt instead of running off."

"I couldn't."

"Now, listen to me real carefully, Junior. Are you listening?"

He nodded.

"Get your face out of my skirt." She pulled the cloth away. "Junior, open your eyes."

Junior squinted.

"You have a telephone, don't you?"

He nodded.

"Go up to the house. Dial the operator. Tell the operator that you need the ambulance."

Junior nodded.

"Tell her what your name is and where you live. Can you do that, Junior? This is real important."

"What are you going to do?"

"I'm going to see if I can help your grandfather. Now go on. Hurry."

Junior took a few backward steps, and then he turned and, once again, ran up the hill to the house.

Michael and Vern came around the bend. They were at the very spot where Pap had thrown them the rope.

"He's still there," Michael said, "I see his feet."

Vern did not answer. "But there's somebody with him," Michael went on. "It's that old lady."

Michael stopped pulling at his clothes. He had been trying to prepare himself for that awful moment when his mother laid eyes on him. Now he stood still too.

"I wonder where Junior is," he said.

Vern shook his head.

"Maybe he went for help."

Vern lifted his shivering shoulders and let them fall.

"Anyway, I don't think he's dead, because she wouldn't be working on him, would she?"

Vern didn't answer.

"Why don't you yell and ask if he's all right?"

Vern shook his head.

"Want me to?"

Vern said, "No."

All the way up the creek, Michael had been talking about how various members of his family had fainted exactly the way Pap had fainted, then they had come to and been fine. Finally Vern had allowed himself to believe that was the way it would be with Pap.

"We'll go around the bend," Michael said, "and Junior and Pap will be there together, perfectly all right. They'll be the ones glad to see us!"

Now they had rounded the bend, and the dream was over. Pap lay where he had fallen, and bending over him, like an angel of darkness, was Mad Mary. The fact that she was there somehow made things worse instead of better.

94

And it's my fault, Vern said to himself. This thought had been threatening like a storm for most of the walk, but Vern had allowed Michael's hopeful tales to hold it off. Now the storm broke.

It's my fault. If I had not made the raft, Pap wouldn't be . . . He couldn't even think the word.

He wrapped his arms around his chest.

"You want me to come home with you?" Michael asked. "Or maybe I should go home and get my mom. Would that be better? Maybe the rescue squad. What do you think?"

If only I had not made the raft . . . Why did I do that? Why didn't I—

Michael touched Vern's arm. "What do you think?"

"About what?"

"About whether I should go get my mom."

For the first time in his life, Vern wanted Michael's mom's firmness. He ducked his head.

"Does that mean get her or not?"

"Get her."

"If my dad's home, I'll get him too."

Vern lifted his shoulders again and let them fall. He and Michael walked without speaking the half mile to the Houstons' bridge. There Michael spoke again. "My mom'll know what to do."

Vern stepped onto the bridge. He hesitated because he was crossing more than water.

Then Michael said in a lower voice, "Vern, I know he's not dead."

Vern bobbed his head to show he'd heard, and then he started across. Through the cracks between the boards, he could see the water had already begun to recede.

If only I had seen this bridge, Vern thought, maybe I could have grabbed it. Why didn't I just . . .

Holding himself tighter, he jumped off the bridge and broke into a run for home.

The Long, Long Night

MAGGIE PICKED UP THE PHONE AND SAID "HELLO."

"Maggie, is that you?"

"Yes, it's me."

Maggie sank down onto a chair, directly in the blast from the window air conditioner.

"Who is this, Vern or Junior?" Maggie had never been able to tell their voices apart over the telephone.

"It's Vern."

"Vern, I am so glad you called. I am all by myself in this motel room and I am going crazy. I—"

"Where's Mom?"

"Give me a chance and I'll tell you. Mom has gone out with some bull rider named Cody Gray."

"When will she be back?"

"How would I know? Late! She does this every night, Vern. I don't even know where they go in that big silver convertible. I can't figure out why Mom wanted me to come if all she was going to do was run off and leave me. Vern——"

Vern interrupted. "Pap had a heart attack."

97

Maggie stopped in mid-sentence. "What?"

"He may die."

The blast from the air conditioner was icy cold. Maggie's knees began to tremble beneath her jeans.

"Pap?"

"Yes."

"How did it happen? When?"

"This afternoon. He was throwing a rope to me and Michael—we were out on the creek in a raft—and after he threw the rope, he just staggered up the bank and fell over. You and Mom better come home."

"We will. But, listen, Vern, don't hang up yet." She sensed Vern was lowering the receiver. "Who's staying with you and Junior?"

"Mary."

"Mad Mary?"

"Yes."

"Let me speak to Junior."

"He's asleep. He was real upset because he was with Pap when it— Oh, I don't want to talk about it anymore. You'll hear all about it when you get home."

"Vern, don't hang up," she said again. Vern was known for his short phone conversations. Most of the time he never even said good-bye. "I've got to hear more about this. Did you talk to the doctor—"

She heard a dial tone. After a long minute, she put the phone back in its cradle.

She got up slowly and looked around the room as if she'd forgotten what she was doing there. Then, in a robotlike way, she began to get her clothes and put them in her suitcase. She packed her mom's clothes in the same slow way.

She glanced around the room to make sure she wasn't leaving anything. Then she went out and sat on the edge of a rusty lounge chair by the blue swimming pool.

People swam in the pool, got out, dried off, drank beer at the tables. Cars moved in and out of the parking lot. Late arrivals checked into the Bar None and found their rooms. Maggie noticed none of this.

She sat tensely, her arms wrapped around her knees, bathed in the red glow of the motel sign and the amber glow of the Bar-B-Q Barn. Her eyes watched the vacancy sign because that was where cars turned in from the highway.

At two thirty in the morning Cody's silver Cadillac convertible pulled into the motel drive.

Maggie got to her feet instantly. She crossed the parking lot. Cody's convertible stopped in front of room 104, taking up two slots. The motor was idling.

Neither her mother nor Cody noticed her. Her mother was kissing Cody good night when Maggie opened the car door.

The moon was high and full. The stars were out. A night breeze blew from the west.

Mad Mary was sitting on the porch, in the swing. It was after midnight, but Mary couldn't sleep under a roof. Anyway, she loved the night sky. On nights like this she felt she could, with her naked eye, see stars scientists hadn't even thought about.

She heard a knock on the front door. She knew it had to be Junior. No one else would knock to come out of a house.

"Come on out, Junior," she said, "and join me."

Junior came out on the porch in his mother's pajamas. These were the pajamas he had packed so happily that morning for the spend-the-night.

His feet padded across the uneven plank flooring, and Junior took his place in the swing. He sat as close as he could to Mary, and she put her arm around his shoulder. She began to pat him in rhythm with the swing. "I thought you were asleep," she said.

"I kept having bad dreams."

"Well, sit out here and keep me company."

"All right, if you want me to."

"Look at the stars, Junior. That'll make you feel better. It does me."

"All right." He would watch the stars if she wanted him to, but the only thing that made him feel better was being close to her.

Junior took a deep breath, inhaling her comforting woodsy smell. They watched the sky without speaking for a few minutes. Then Junior broke the silence.

"Did your grandfather ever almost die?" he asked.

"He did die," Mary said. "I was just about your age when it happened too."

"Did you see it happen?"

"Yes, I did. As a matter of fact, I was holding his hand."

"You were?" Junior pulled back to look at her.

"In those days, Junior, it seemed important to be with somebody when they died. The whole family was there, standing around my grandfather's bed. Folks don't do that much anymore." She glanced down at Junior's moonlit face and changed the subject. "Your grandfather and I were in a school show one time. Did he ever tell you about that? He did rope tricks and I sang 'Ave Maria.' "

100

Junior blinked his eyes. "He told me you sang, but not which song. Do you still know it?"

She shook her head. "My singing days are over, Junior."

"Could you hum a little bit?"

She hummed a tune Junior had never heard before. Even when she was humming, she couldn't make the high notes. When she stopped, Junior said, "That was nice."

There was another of those long, comforting pauses. Junior cleared his throat. "Getting back to the subject of grandfathers . . . when your grandfather died, did it scare you?" he asked.

"No, Junior, it didn't, but I was expecting him to die. My mother had a long talk with me before we went—about how Poppa Dear—that's what we called him—Poppa Dear was dying and what I was supposed to do and how I was to behave."

"I wish my mother had told me what to do," Junior said. Mary hugged him.

"If you don't want to talk about it," Junior said, "that's all right, but I'd like to hear some more."

"Let's see. We went in the bedroom, and, Junior, my grandfather's bedroom was bigger than a lot of churches, and when we got over to the bed, it just happened that I was standing right by his hand. I don't know why, but I reached out and took it. His eyes weren't open, but for a while he held my hand back. Then all of a sudden, he just let go. That was how I knew he was gone."

"Oh."

"Anyway," she went on in a different, firmer tone of voice, "don't you let folks dying do to you what it did to me."

"What?"

"Drive you away from people, make you go off and live by yourself in a cave."

"Oh, I wouldn't do that," Junior said. "I couldn't. I'd miss people too much."

Mary hugged him again. "You've had about as bad a day as a boy your age can have, haven't you?"

Junior rested his head on Mary's shoulder. "I sure hope so," he said.

Going Home

"WELL, I NEVER THOUGHT PAP WOULD DO SOMETHING like this to me," Vicki Blossom said. She and Maggie were in the car, on their way home to Alderson. They had passed through a dust storm, and the windshield wipers were still wiping away the dust.

"Mom, he didn't *do* anything to you. He had a heart attack!"

"Well, you know what I mean."

"No, I don't know what you mean. You act like he did it on purpose to stop you from having fun with Cody Gray!"

Vicki Blossom began driving faster, weaving in and out of interstate traffic. On either side of the highway were stretches of flat ground. Behind them the dust storm reached to the sky.

By evening the oil towers they were passing would have changed to trees. The brown fields would be green hills. By early morning they would be home.

Maggie blinked her eyes. She had been trying to cry ever since she had opened the convertible door and said, "Pap's had a heart attack."

"How bad?"

"I don't know."

Everything happened in a rush then. Her mother was out of the convertible, hugging her, crying, "Oh, no, not Pap. Oh—Junior and Vern. We got to pack."

"I already did."

Cody's hand was on Vicki's shoulder. "What you want me to do, hon? How can I help?"

"Oh, I don't know. I can't think."

"I'll check you out of the motel. I'll look after Sandy Boy. You just throw your bags in the car and go."

In five minutes Maggie was in the car. Through the window she could see Cody Gray pressing some money into her mom's hand.

"I can't take that, Cody."

"Now, I don't want to worry about you," he said. "That car of yours is liable to quit. If it does, you rent another one and keep going."

"I'll pay you back."

"You just take care of yourself. I don't want anything happening to you." He leaned down to look at Maggie through the car window. "You either, little lady."

Then he straightened. "I'm real, real sorry." There was a pause. Maggie looked in the sideview mirror. They were kissing.

"I'll see you," Cody said, "in—let's see—Phoenix."

"Oh, I hope so."

"I'm counting on it."

"Come on, Mom!"

Her mom got in the car, and they pulled out of the motel. Her mom held on to Cody's hand out the window until they got past the swimming pool. "You taking me

105

with you?" He laughed. Vicki Blossom let go and laughed too.

The whole thing made Maggie try even harder to cry.

The dust was gone now, so Vicki Blossom turned off the window wipers. "It just seems like yesterday when I first saw Pap," she said as she passed a six-wheeler. "I met Pap before I met your dad, did you know that? It was at the Snake River Stampede in Nampa, Idaho."

"I knew you met at a rodeo. I didn't know which one."

"The Snake River Stampede. Pap introduced me to your dad on a Monday, and I married him two weeks later on a Saturday. I would have married him sooner, but he was slow in asking." She smiled slightly. "The wedding was at the Pikes-Peak-or-Bust Rodeo in Colorado Springs. The bride wore white—a white satin shirt, and so did the groom."

"I knew you got married at a rodeo, but I didn't know which one."

"I had an old Ford in those days and we sold it for three hundred dollars, hooked my horse trailer up to their pickup, and took off—Pap and your dad and me. That was probably the happiest summer of my life."

Maggie rubbed her eyes. They were so dry they hurt. She was watching her mother. When she was sure her mother was finished talking about her courtship, she said, "I wish there was no such thing as heart attacks."

"You know what Pap told me after your dad died? I never will forget this. When your dad died, Pap was the saddest person I have ever seen in my life. Oh, we were all broken up about it, but it was like Pap wouldn't ever get over it—and the truth is, he never did."

They drove on in silence for a few miles. Maggie waited. Finally she said, "So, go on. What did Pap say?"

Vicki looked at her blankly.

"You were getting ready to tell me something that Pap said after my daddy died."

"Oh, I was thinking about something else."

"Cody Gray?" Maggie asked.

"No, not Cody Gray. Give me a break, Maggie. Pap said that when he was little, life was like a giant seesaw, and everybody he knew was down on one end with him. He said he didn't even know one single dead person. No one was on the other end. Well, then his little sister died, then an aunt, then another aunt. When he was seventeen, his mom died.

"Pretty soon, Pap said, the seesaw was just about balanced. He knew about as many people on one end as he did on the other. When your dad died, though, Pap said the seesaw tipped, the other end went down so hard, so fast, Pap said it almost pulled him down there too."

"I'm only twelve and my seesaw's already balanced," Maggie said. "A lot of people I love have died. If Pap dies too . . ." She couldn't finish.

"What we need to do is pile some more people on our end—get some new friends, have some fun."

"I don't want Pap to die." Maggie felt tears come to her eyes. With relief she wiped them on the hem of her shirt.

"I don't either." Vicki Blossom smiled sadly. "Nobody ever wants a Blossom to die. You know how sometimes people will say, 'Isn't it a blessing that so and so passed on,' well, nobody ever says that about a Blossom. And you know something else?" She blew the horn at an eighteen-wheeler. "Nobody ever will."

107

In the Shadows with Mud

MUD WAS IN THE SHELTER OF THE PINE TREES. HE HAD been there, sitting uneasily on his haunches for hours. From time to time, his whole body trembled.

Mud didn't understand what had happened. One moment he had been bounding down the hill, ears flapping, tail flying, barking with excitement. He had just flushed a pair of flickers out of the grass.

At that triumphant moment, he had seen Pap with his rope. There was something about Pap slinging a rope around his head that always sent Mud into a special frenzy.

This time the excitement was heightened by all the screaming. Something big was happening at the creek. Mud wanted to get in on the action.

He arrived at the creek bank when Pap's loop was whizzing in the air. Mud never took his eyes off it. Usually Pap had to calm him down with soft-spoken commands. "Take it easy, Mud. I'm not doing this for your amusement. No jumping. You've seen ropes before. Give me room."

This time Pap didn't say any of those things. His eyes

watched something in the middle of the creek. Pap was intent.

Before Mud could see what had Pap's attention, Pap stepped into the water. Instantly Mud did too. Pap threw the rope. Mud barked.

The rope seemed to fly like the flickers, in one long graceful arch. Then the rope landed, and Mud splashed into the creek, bent on retrieving it.

He swam. The current carried him swiftly downstream.

He crawled out. He shook himself. He ran back. As far as he was concerned, the action was still in the middle of the creek. He plunged into the water.

Again the current carried him downstream. He swam to the bank and climbed out. He shook himself and barked at the boys now disappearing around the bend.

Still barking, he ran back to Pap for instructions. He got there just as Pap stumbled up the bank. Pap grabbed a tree. Then with a sigh so low only Mud's keen ears heard it, Pap slumped to the ground.

All this had been one wild, glorious moment for Mud. Now he stopped in his tracks.

Pap did not move. Mud didn't move either.

The moment was frozen in time. Junior was in one place, Mud in another. Both of them concentrated on Pap.

Junior made the first move. He went over and started talking to Pap in a low, pleading voice. Junior was crying.

Mud's tail slowly sagged between his legs. He stood statue-still. A worried crease came in his forehead.

Then Junior started yelling. He got up and walked backward, stumbling. He would have stepped on Mud if Mud had not dodged out of his way. Junior's movements were so wild, so scary, that Mud finally ran to the truck and got between the front tires.

In the shelter of the truck, Mud began to pant. He shifted his worried gaze from Junior to Pap, back to Junior. From time to time he gave a sharp, anxious bark.

Now Junior was running. Mud moved back further under the truck. This time Junior kept running, all the way to the top of the hill and out of sight.

Mud hesitated for a moment. Then he came out. Keeping low to the ground, he crawled toward Pap.

Ten feet away from Pap he came to a halt. He did not want to go any farther. He was still crouched in that same spot, whining, when Mad Mary came over the hill.

"Shoo!" she said. She waved her cane. "Git!"

Normally Mud would have growled—he had never liked the wild way Mad Mary smelled. He didn't trust anybody who smelled wild. Once he had even tried to attack her.

"Shoo! I said, 'Git!' "

This time, Mud ran for the trees. He ran in a crouch, as if he had just received a powerful kick, as if more had gone out of him than just his instinct to chase Mad Mary.

He went deep into the woods, running hard. Then he circled around, and came back to the pines. This was the highest spot on the Blossoms' farm.

Mud stood there, hidden in the shadows, sides heaving, watching with his golden eyes. The ambulance came, siren wailing. Pap was carried up the creek, over the bridge, and loaded into the ambulance. Then the ambulance drove away.

All this brought a double furrow to Mud's brow. It was as deep as if it had been carved with a knife.

Time passed, but not for Mud. He kept standing in the trees, tail between his legs. Every time something new happened—like a strange woman bringing food, he watched intently, but the furrow between his brows never eased.

Finally dark came. The lights went off in the house. Mud watched by moonlight.

At ten o'clock Mud began to howl. Mud was a good howler. On one of his better nights, he could be heard for miles.

This time Mud's howling was different. His howls were low, quiet, more like moans. They were so low that the people at the house never heard them above the rush of the creek.

Mud howled for a long time, his sharp nose pointing to the moon. About midnight, he began to shiver. It wasn't because he was still wet from the creek, or that he was cold . . .

The shivers made him want to be in his misery hole.

Mud moved toward the house. He kept his distance, like a fox scouting a chicken house. The house was dark and quiet, but someone was in the swing on the porch.

Mud stopped.

It was Mad Mary. He could smell her. It was the wild smell that usually brought up his hunting instinct, but that was gone. He was not the same dog who had flushed the flickers that afternoon and barked triumphantly as the birds wheeled into the sky. Tonight he only wanted to get in his hole.

He went to the back of the house and nosed his way through the thick shrubbery. Then, in a sort of tunnel he had created over the years, he made his way to the front porch.

He did not make a sound. He did not rustle a leaf.

"I smell wet dog," Mad Mary said, but the rhythm of her swinging did not stop.

With his tail between his legs, Mud slipped behind the steps. There was his misery hole at last.

He turned around several times, circling as usual so that his body would be perfectly positioned. Then with a sigh he dropped his body into his dusty, well-worn misery hole.

The Misery Hole

"TELL ME AGAIN," JUNIOR BEGGED.

"Junior, I've told you ten times."

"Just once more."

"And then you'll stop asking?"

"I'll try to."

Vicki Blossom said, "All right, but this is the last time."

Junior leaned forward eagerly.

The Blossom family was on the front porch. Vicki Blossom was in a rocking chair. Maggie and Vern were on the steps. Junior was balanced on the porch railing in front of his mother.

"Pap is alive," his mother recited. "He is lying in a bed in room 328. He is making the nurses' lives miserable."

"I want to see him," Junior said.

"Junior, I explained that. You can talk to him on the phone tomorrow—maybe."

"I need to see him."

"Junior——"

"I need to!"

"Junior, don't you believe me when I tell you Pap's alive?"

"I'm trying to."

Vicki Blossom sighed.

Maggie watched her mom critically. Ever since she and her mom had gotten home, she had felt like the oldest one in the family, the mother. The hatred she had felt for her mom in the Bar None Motel was gone, but a nagging irritation lingered. "Mom, the reason he can't believe it is because the last time he saw Pap, Pap looked dead."

"Well, I know that," Vickie Blossom said.

Maggie turned away and pretended to be interested in the sunset.

"It sure is quiet around here," Vicki Blossom said suddenly. "Where are the dogs?"

"Mom, you're as bad as Junior," Maggie snapped. "We've told you ten times. Mud is under the porch in his misery hole. Dump got bit by a snake."

"How did that happen? I forget."

"Well, he was under the house," Junior said at once, "and he got bit and he ran off in the woods. Remember? Pap was telling me about his dog getting snake-bit when . . ."

"I wish I had a misery hole," Vicki Blossom said. "I'd crawl in it myself right about now." She lifted her hair up from her neck. "You know, this whole thing's just beginning to hit me. There was so much to do—driving home, making sure Pap's insurance was all right. I haven't had time to think till right this minute. Make room for me, Mud!"

"I'll check under the porch," Maggie said, "and see if he's still there."

114

Maggie went down the steps and peered under the porch. "He's still here."

"Well, drag him out. He can be miserable up here with the rest of us."

"Come on, Mud."

Mud was curled into a tight ball. His eyes were shut. His nose was dry. His face had a sunken look. From time to time his shoulders trembled. He had been here like this for two and a half days.

"Come on, Mud." Maggie tugged gently at his bandana. Mud didn't open his eyes.

Maggie thought about bodily pulling him out, but there was something formal in the way he had curled himself away from the world that stopped her.

"He doesn't want to come, Mom."

"You know what he probably does? He lies under there while we're home so we'll feel sorry for him. Then the minute we're gone, he comes out and tools around."

"I don't think so," Maggie said. "All the food we put is right where we left it. He hasn't touched a thing."

"Give him a piece of ham. That'll bring him out. It sure was nice of Michael's mother, Vern. She sent a Virginia ham and a congealed salad." Vicki Blossom kept rocking, staring over the tops of the trees at the setting sun. "And Ralphie's mom sent a deviled egg platter and two get-well-soon balloons. Everybody's been real nice."

"But she won't let Michael play with me anymore," Vern said. "She thinks I'm a bad influence."

"You are not a bad influence."

"She probably thinks it's my fault that Pap had a heart attack, that if I hadn't made the raft—"

"Vern, listen to me. What happened to Pap was not

115

your fault, and Pap would not want you thinking that it was. That man loves you kids. He wants you to be happy. And right now, the thing you can do to help Pap get out of the hospital is to stop thinking you put him there. I mean it, Vern."

"I'm trying," Vern said.

Maggie came out of the house dangling a slice of ham. She went down the steps and waved it in front of Mud. He didn't open his eyes.

"He's not even interested in ham."

"He did something like this before," Vicki Blossom said. "Remember when Pap got arrested? Mud collapsed in front of a Dairy Queen. Remember that?"

"This is different," Vern said. "Mud thinks Pap's dead."

Vickie Blossom said, "When Mud gets hungry enough, Mud'll eat."

Vern shook his head. "I lifted his eyelid yesterday, and, Mom, I couldn't see his eye at all. It was like, well, he wasn't in there anymore."

"I don't believe that," Junior said. He went down the steps, and Maggie shifted to make room for him.

Junior drew in his breath. Mud seemed worse than he had just that morning when Junior put fresh water in his bowl. Mud reminded Junior of himself that awful afternoon when his head started floating off his body.

Hesitantly Junior reached out his hand. He raised Mud's eyelid. The white showed bloodshot; the golden iris was rolled up into Mud's head.

"Pap's not dead," he told the unseeing eye. "I thought he was, too, but now I think he's not."

Mud did not move.

116

"I would never lie to you, Mud. Pap is alive."

"Save your breath," Vicki Blossom said.

At nine o'clock the next morning Dump limped into the Blossoms' yard on three legs. His left hind leg was swollen. The skin beneath the much-licked fur was red.

Junior was out on the porch steps, having a one-sided conversation with Mud. "Mud," he was saying, "I'm going to get to talk to him on the phone, but I can't bring the phone out here. The line won't reach. You just have to believe me. You just have to!"

Just then Junior caught sight of Dump. He jumped to his feet.

"Mom! Everybody!" he called as he ran. "Dump's back!"

"Yippee," his mom said flatly from the kitchen.

Junior wanted to throw his arms around the dog, but he was afraid he'd hurt him. His hands fluttered over Dump. Finally he scratched him behind the ear with one finger.

"I'll go get you something to eat," he said. He ran to the steps and picked up the slice of ham. "I'm going to borrow this," he told Mud. Then he ran across the yard, dusting the ham off on his pants. "Here," he said.

Dump ate the ham out of Junior's hand, and then he licked Junior's palm.

"You're just in time to help," Junior told him. "Mud's under the house and he won't come out. He may even be dying. See, he thinks Pap is dead, and I've told him and told him that Pap's alive, but he won't listen. If anybody can get him out, it's you. Come on. Hurry as fast as you possibly can."

Dear Maggie

RALPHIE WAS COMPOSING A LETTER TO MAGGIE. HE FRE-
quently started letters to her, but he never mailed them.

His mother passed behind him. "Are you actually writing a letter?" she asked. Quickly Ralphie turned the paper
over, facedown on the table.

"I can write a letter if I want to," he said.

"I'm surprised because I remember I had to physically
threaten you to make you write your birthday thank-you
notes."

"That was because I got underwear."

"You did not get underwear. And last week I watched
you in complete misery because your teacher made you
write to an author."

"And then I didn't get to send it," Ralphie said.

"Perhaps that was because it started out, 'I haven't read
any of your books, because your titles stink."

"Mom! You read over my shoulder."

He waited, arms crossed over the sheet of paper, until
she went out of the room. Then he turned the sheet of
paper over. "Dear Maggie," he read.

He paused and scratched his head with the end of his ballpoint pen.

"Ralphie, I asked you to help me with the balloons," his mother called from the bedroom. Ralphie's mother had a business called The Balloonerie. "I cannot get twenty-one balloons into the back of the station wagon and put on a clown suit at the same time."

"Mom, I'm writing a letter. You saw that."

"The letter can wait."

Ralphie sighed. He got up from the table. "My next letter will be to the Society for the Prevention of Cruelty to Children."

"Put the four 'Smile, it's a nice day' balloons in first. Those are my last deliveries. Then the fourteen 'Happy Birthdays'—they're for a party. Last to go in will be the Mickey Mouse, the Snoopy, and the 'You're somebody special.'"

"No Drop Dead's?"

"I will be glad when you learn to drive, Ralphie, so you can deliver balloons."

"I'll be glad when I can drive too," he said.

Delivering balloons, he had already figured out, would give him the perfect excuse to stop by Maggie's. "Oh, I had some balloon deliveries out this way," he would say. Never mind that country people never had balloons delivered. Then he could add, "Want to ride along?"

Of course he would have to wear a clown suit, his mother would insist on that, but still it would be nice to be alone in the car with Maggie.

Ralphie put the balloons in the station wagon and came back to the kitchen table. Beneath "Dear Maggie" he wrote, "I'm sorry about Pap's heart attack."

His mom came back into the kitchen in her clown suit and red wig. She claimed to have worked out her own individual clown makeup, but she looked a lot like Ronald McDonald.

Ralphie wasn't going to wear makeup no matter what— maybe, *maybe* he would stick one of those red balls on his nose right before a customer opened the front door, but that would be it.

Ralphie heard his mom's station wagon start, and he raised his head to watch her pull out into the street. Then the balloons blocked his mom from view as she drove away.

The phone rang. Ralphie did not get up. He called, "Phone's ringing," to his brother. "Mom said for you to answer the phone while she was gone."

"She did not," the brother called back.

"All right, if you don't believe me, don't answer."

"I won't."

"Only it's probably a balloon order. This first thing mom's going to ask you when she gets home is—"

The brother picked up the phone on the next ring. He came into the kitchen.

"It's for you." He sneered. "It's a girl."

Ralphie jumped up so quickly, his chair tipped over backward.

He grabbed for the phone. There was only one girl in the world who could be calling him.

"Hello."

"Ralphie?"

It was Maggie, and it sounded as if she were crying. Ralphie hated for Maggie to cry. He was in love with her, had been for two years, since that first electric moment he opened his eyes in the hospital and saw her sitting on the foot of Junior's hospital bed. Even if she hadn't been telling the story of how she had her brother busted into city jail, he would have loved her.

"Yes, it's me. What's wrong?"

"Oh, Ralphie."

"What? What is it?"

"You remember Mud?"

"Mud, the dog?"

"Yes."

"What about him?"

"Well, he's dying."

"Oh."

Ralphie knew from the way she said the words that that wasn't the worst of it. More was coming. His shoulders straightened. He knew too that somehow what was coming would directly involve him.

"And, Ralphie."

"Yes."

"Ralphie."

There was an extra syllable in his name this time.

"Yes! Go ahead. I'm ready."

"Ralphie, we think we know how to save him."

Ralphie hated to ask, but he knew he had to. "How?"

"We have to smuggle him into the hospital so that he can see Pap's still alive."

"Wait a minute. Mud is the big dog or the little fuzzy fellow?"

"The big one. And, Ralphie, there's a problem."

"Oh, really."

"Yes, Mud won't walk. He's in a coma."

121

Her voice began to tremble again. Ralphie wished it wouldn't do that.

"See, if Pap's dead, Mud doesn't want to live either, but Pap's not dead. It's like an old-timey play I saw on TV where the boy died because he thought the girl he loved was dead, and then she came to, and he really was dead."

"I missed that one."

There was a silence, and Maggie said, "If you'd rather not . . ."

"No, I want to," Ralphie said. "I haven't done anything illegal in a while. I'm losing my touch."

"Oh, Ralphie, I can always count on you."

"It looks that way. When do you want the smuggling to take place?"

"Tonight. Tomorrow may be, you know, too late."

"Tonight," Ralphie said.

He set the phone onto the receiver. He put one hand on his letter and crumpled it into a ball.

"What did she want?" Ralphie's brother asked.

"She wants me to smuggle her dog into the hospital to visit her grandfather."

"Tell me the truth," the brother said in disgust. "You always lie! Tell the truth!"

Smuggling Mud

RALPHIE SIGHED.

Beneath his mother's clown suit, his heart was pumping hard.

"Are you sure this dog's alive?" he asked.

Mud had been pulled out of his misery hole. He now lay in the moonlight in front of the steps, apparently dead.

Maggie, Vern, and Junior were on one side of him. Ralphie was on the other. All four leaned over Mud, looking for signs of life.

Maggie said, "Yes."

Ralphie said, "I just don't want to go to the trouble of smuggling a dead dog into Alderson General Hospital, that's all."

"He's not dead," Junior confirmed. "If you look real close you can see his heart beating between his ribs."

"I don't see any heart beating."

"Right there."

Junior pointed with one dirty finger to a spot three inches below Mud's bandana.

Maggie said, "Yes, it is beating, Ralphie."

Ralphie said, "He could be brain-dead." A cool silence followed this remark. Ralphie tried to put his hands in his pockets and discovered the clown suit didn't have pockets.

He said, "Oh, all right. I give up. Let's get him into the wagon."

"Wait a minute. We need a quilt," Maggie said.

"We need a lifting crane," Ralphie muttered.

Maggie pretended not to hear. She ran quietly up the porch steps, opened the screen door without a sound, and disappeared into the house.

"I hope she doesn't wake up Mom," Vern said.

"I hope she does," Ralphie said. "I'm sure your mom would get a kick out of me standing here in my mom's clown suit with two get-well-soon balloons tied to my wrist, getting ready to pull a dead dog to town."

"I like you in your clown suit," Junior said. "You make a good clown."

Ralphie did not respond.

"You could be in a circus."

"I am not wearing this clown suit to amuse people, Junior. I am wearing this clown suit because the nurses are used to seeing this clown suit bringing balloons to patients."

"I know that."

"This clown suit is a disguise."

"I know that."

"It is—"

Maggie came down the steps silently. She spread a quilt on the ground and rolled Mud on top of it. He gave no resistance.

"All right, let's get him into the wagon."

Ralphie took the head. Vern took the feet. Together they picked up the motionless Mud.

"How much does this dog weigh?" Ralphie asked as they swung Mud into the wagon.

Mud landed with a thud. He did not move.

"I don't know. Fifty pounds," Maggie said. "Sixty at the most. He's lost a lot of weight because he hasn't eaten in three days."

"You couldn't prove it by me," Ralphie said.

Maggie tucked the quilt around Mud and patted it. "He's ready."

Mud lay with curved grace in the wagon. The tip of his tail stuck out from one end of the crazy quilt, his long nose stuck out the other.

Ralphie reached out his hand—the one with the get-well-soon balloons tied on the wrist, and felt the rope that held the wagon to his bicycle.

"Vern's good with knots. Let him do it," Junior had said with brotherly pride. "Vern tied the knots on my wings that time and they wouldn't come off no matter what. The police had to cut them off."

"I didn't do the knots so good on my raft," Vern admitted, stepping forward.

He had brushed his hands together as if he would now make up for the failure of those raft knots. Then he proceeded to tie the biggest knot Ralphie had ever seen in his life. And then he spit on it.

Feeling the hard damp knot, Ralphie knew there was no chance the wagon would come loose and slip mercifully into a ditch along the way, thereby jarring Mud into action. What he wouldn't give to see that dog jump out of the quilt and take a leak on the nearest bush.

"We better get going," Maggie said. "It's a long way to town."

Ralphie didn't move. Being friends with the Blossoms was hard on a person with an artificial leg, he thought, because you were always called on to do things like climb trees and scale mountains and, now, pull a fifty-pound dog to town in a child's wagon.

He rose and threw his good leg over his bicycle.

Maggie said, "Don't go too fast or we won't be able to keep up."

"There is little chance I will go too fast," Ralphie said. He did not add there was a better chance the Blossoms would have to push.

He was on his bicycle now, ready to go. The get-well-soon balloons bobbed over his head.

Beneath the handlebars of his bicycle, he crossed his fingers. "Here goes," he said. He braced his artificial leg to push.

At that moment the porch light went on. Ralphie in his clown suit, Mud in the crazy quilt, and the three Blossom children were lit up as if they had been on a stage. They froze. Only the balloons over Ralphie's head continued to bob.

Vicki Blossom stepped onto the porch.

"And just what is going on here?" she said.

Led by a Clown

"I CANNOT BELIEVE I AM DOING THIS," VICKI BLOSSOM said.

She was standing outside the emergency exit of the hospital with Mud in her arms.

"Mom, you're doing a wonderful thing," Maggie said. "We would never have made it if you hadn't driven us. I'm really proud of you."

"Well, I'm not proud of myself," Vicki said. She shifted Mud into a better position. "You know what's going to happen? Some nurse is going to see me with this quilt and think I'm bringing an injured child to the hospital and she's going to rush me into the emergency room and I'm going to have to put the quilt down and they'll see this—" She looked down at Mud's long nose with distaste. "This creature! Then what am I going to say?"

"I'll go first, Mrs. Blossom." Ralphie stepped forward. "I'll make sure the halls are clear."

"I am so furious with this dog," Vicki Blossom said.

"Mom, he can't help it."

"I think he can." Again she looked down at Mud. "I

want to tell you one thing, Mud, and I know you can hear me. I know that little pea-brain is working. You owe me for this. You really—"

"The coast is clear!" Ralphie said.

He held the door open. With gratitude he watched Vicki Blossom step through. That could have been him.

He ran across the hall. "Hold it," he told them.

He peered around the corner. When he saw the hall was empty, he said, "The elevators are this way."

"I thought they were in the lobby," Vicki Blossom said.

"Mrs. Blossom, we're taking the service elevator."

"Mom, listen to Ralphie," Maggie said. "He knows this hospital."

They hurried to the service elevator. The door was open. Ralphie had already pushed the HOLD button. The doors slid smoothly shut behind them.

"I can't believe this is happening to me," Vicki Blossom said as the elevator rose to the third floor.

The doors opened and Ralphie pushed HOLD again. "Let me check." He stepped into the hall. "Coast is clear. Come on."

At the water fountain he held them back again. They were used to stopping on command now.

Ralphie went around the corner alone. There was one nurse at the nurse's station. Ralphie grinned when he recognized her. He said, "Hi, remember me?"

"Ralphie?"

"In person."

"What in the world are you doing here?"

"Delivering balloons."

"At this hour?"

128

"Well, my mom is. I just wanted to say hello to Mr. Blossom."

"Oh, no, you don't. Mr. Blossom has been out of the cardiac unit one day, and you are not going in there with any balloons."

A buzzer sounded behind her, and a voice on the intercom asked, "Is it time for my sleeping pill? If you don't come soon, I'll be asleep."

"I'm coming, Mr. May. You'll have to excuse me, Ralphie."

"Oh, sure. No problem. I've got to be going anyway."

The nurse disappeared down the hall with a tray, and Ralphie signaled the Blossoms.

Silently they moved around the corner and down the hall. "This is his room," Vicki Blossom said at the door to 328.

Ralphie pushed open the door, and he and the Blossoms slipped inside.

They waited against the door, nobody saying anything. The light was dim. They tried to make out the forms in the four beds.

"That's his bed," Vicki whispered. She led the way to the one by the window.

There were sides on the bed to keep Pap from rolling out. Vicki Blossom raised Mud's body high enough to drop him over the top. She sighed with relief.

Mud landed beside Pap with a soft thud. The quilt fell open. Mud's nose was pointing toward Pap's pillow, his tail to the foot of the bed. His legs were curled against Pap's side. He did not move.

"Pap," Vicki Blossom said.

Pap snored softly.

Vern said, "He's not going to wake up."

They waited. The Blossoms were crowded so closely around the bed they could hear each other breathing.

Junior cleared his throat. "Pap, Mud and me are here. We wanted to see if you were—" He broke off, then added, "all right" in a firm voice.

"Pap," Maggie said. Pap did not move, and she looked up at her mother for advice. "Should we wake him up or what?"

"I don't know," Vicki Blossom said. "I can't believe this is happening to me. I have carried this dog halfway across the county for nothing. Pap is not going to wake up—I'm not even sure we should wake him up. He might have another heart attack. Then where would we be? And now I'm going to have to carry this dog back to the car! I cannot believe this!"

"I'll carry him part of the way," Ralphie offered. Maggie gave him a look of gratitude. He gave her an it's-nothing shrug.

At that moment, Pap stirred beneath his covers. He turned toward them.

Vicki Blossom reached out and grabbed the two nearest Blossom children—Vern and Junior. They all stopped breathing.

Pap's hand fumbled restlessly across the white spread. His fingers touched Mud's ear. Then his hand made one more move and covered Mud's head like a cap.

There was a long moment while nothing happened. Pap didn't move again. Mud didn't move either.

And then Mud's eyes flickered open.

He blinked.

His eyes rolled up to where Pap's familiar hand rested on his brow.

Mud opened his mouth in a long yawn. His tongue curled out of his mouth. He struggled to turn over in the tight space between Pap and the side of the bed.

He looked long and hard at Pap's face. He rubbed his face against the stiff bedspread. A whine of pleasure began deep in his chest. His tail thumped against the bed railing.

He began pulling himself toward Pap's face. His long legs stretched out behind him, pushing him forward.

"Oh, we got to get him out of here," Vicki Blossom said. "You know Mud. He's going to start barking. Next thing you know he'll want to run around in circles. Come on!"

She reached into the hospital bed. "Help me, somebody!"

Ralphie reached in with her. "I'll do that. I'm taller." He realized for the first time this was true. He hoped Maggie was watching.

He pulled Mud manfully into his arms. Mud struggled like a wild animal, but Ralphie held on. This was what love did to a man, he thought, gave him supernatural powers. Over his head, the get-well-soon balloons danced on their strings.

"I'll get his feet," Maggie offered. She reached in and grabbed Mud's hind legs and held them together.

"No problem," Ralphie said.

Mud was doing the dog paddle with his front feet, trying to get to Pap. "Sorry, Pal," Ralphie told him. He could feel the dog's hot eager breath through his clown suit. "Fun's over for the night."

Vicki Blossom peered out the door. "Come on," she said.

The Blossom children ran down the hall. Ralphie and Maggie took the lead. Ralphie was hobbling so fast that his artificial leg seemed like something a person would snap on for extra speed.

Mud gave a sharp bark of protest as they passed the nurse's station. The nurse stuck her head out a doorway to see what was happening.

"Ralphie! What are you doing with that dog? Ralphie! Come back here."

Ralphie ran to the elevator and jabbed the button with his elbow. Mud was digging at Ralphie with his paws. Mud was a good digger, but Ralphie was a man.

In the distance, Ralphie heard the nurse coming closer. His heart was pounding so hard that he didn't hear the hum of the approaching elevator.

The doors surprised him by sliding open. "Everybody on," he said coolly.

He stepped inside. The Blossoms did too.

"Ralphie!" the nurse said.

"Just passing through," he explained as the doors closed on her startled face.

The elevator moved down to the lobby, and Mud threw back his head and howled.

Five-card Stud

Mud barked at the screen door.

The Blossom family was at the supper table. Nobody got up to let him in.

He barked again.

This time Junior got up with a sigh and went to the door. He was eating a chicken leg.

"There is no need to open the door, Junior," Maggie said. "Mud doesn't want to come in. He wants somebody to drive him to the hospital to see Pap again."

Through the screen Mud watched Junior hopefully. Junior opened the door. Mud barked again and backed up in the direction of the car.

Junior said, "No, Mud, you can't go back to the hospital. Mom won't take you."

"That's for sure," Vicki Blossom said.

"And I'm not allowed to drive."

Junior came back to the table. Vicki Blossom waited until he was seated. Then she said, "Guess what we're going to do this summer, kids?"

All the Blossom kids looked at her, but nobody answered.

"Aren't you even going to guess?" she went on. "Don't you want to know?"

Junior couldn't help himself. "I do," he said.

"Well, this summer, soon as school's out, we are going to get in the car and go on the circuit. We're going to have the best time we ever had in our lives. We're going to eat when we're hungry and sleep when we're tired. We're not going to do one single thing we don't feel like doing."

"Will Pap be able to go too?" Junior asked. "I wouldn't want to go without Pap."

"Yes, Pap's going too." She paused and swallowed. "Then, in the fall . . ."

She stopped completely. She put her lips together in the straightest line any of them had ever seen. Finally Junior couldn't stand the suspense.

"What are we going to do in the fall?" he asked.

"In the fall, we're going to settle down."

All three children looked at their mom in astonishment. That was the last thing they had expected.

"Settle down? Us?" Maggie asked.

"Yes, now don't ask me how, because I don't know how yet. I'm going to have to work it out. I could start a riding school—I've thought about that. You could help with the little kids."

It was Maggie's reaction she was watching for. When she saw it, she said defensively, "I mean it, Maggie. I'm going to do it."

"I believe you," Junior said.

"Anyway," she went on, "we don't have to worry about

134

the details now. All we have to concentrate on is having a summer we'll remember all our lives."

"And when we settle down," Junior said, catching her enthusiasm for the new life, "I can spend the night with Mary a lot, can't I?"

"If she'll have you."

"And Maggie can see Ralphie all the time and Vern can see Michael!"

"If his mom'll let me," Vern said gloomily.

"She will," Junior said confidently. He turned his delighted face from Maggie to Vern, then back to his mom. He was aware that Maggie and Vern didn't look as happy as he did—Maggie looked almost suspicious, but they would see. It would work out. It always did.

Vicki Blossom got to her feet. She went into the living room and came back with her purse. She took out an envelope.

"I don't know whether I ought to show you these or not," she said.

"I want to see, no matter what," Junior said.

Maggie said, "Show us what?"

"Well, when I was going through Pap's things, looking for his insurance papers, I came across his old camera. There was film in it. Pap used to take a lot of pictures, remember, but he stopped the day your dad died."

Vicki looked down at the envelope. "Twenty-four Hour Service," it said.

"So I took the roll of film out of the camera and I took it to the drug store. The man didn't know whether the film would still be good after all this time, but he said he'd try."

"Did they come out?"

Vicki opened the envelope and laid the pictures on the

table. There were ten of them. Junior in his dad's hat, Maggie on his shoulders, Vern and his dad playing poker on a picnic table, Vicki and Cotton laughing, some shots of the five of them . . .

"We look so young," Maggie said, picking one up to look at it more closely.

"We were young," Vicki Blossom said.

They passed the pictures around the table.

"I remember this one being taken," Junior said. "At the last minute, right before Pap took the picture, Dad switched hats with me. That's why I have on the big hat and he has on the little one."

"It would be nice if Pap was in some of them," Vicki said.

"He's not *in* them," Junior said, "but he's *part* of them. We wouldn't have these pictures if it wasn't for Pap. Can I have this one of me and Dad to keep?"

"Can I have this one?" Maggie asked.

Vern had already picked out the poker picture.

"Let's see. There are ten. Each of you can have three. I want this one." She slipped out the one of her and Cotton. "Now," she said, "did I do right in showing them to you? Do you feel better or worse?"

"Better!" Junior said.

Maggie thought about it. "Better."

Vern nodded.

Vern was on his absolute best behavior. Michael had called early that morning to say that the ban had been lifted. Vern could come over for two hours.

Vern had run the whole way.

From the minute he entered the kitchen, however, he

was aware that the friendship was on probation. "I've got my eye on both of you," was the way Michael's mother greeted him.

After she went out of the kitchen at last, Michael asked, "What do you want to do?"

"I don't know. What can we do?"

"I don't know."

Vern went over the possibilities in his mind. He had to come up with something so safe, so uncontroversial, that even Michael's mother could not find fault with it.

He straightened. "Do you know how to play poker?"

Michael shook his head.

"You want to learn?"

Michael nodded.

"We'll play for matches. My dad taught me to play. It's been a long time since I played, but it's coming back to me. Where are your cards?"

"In the game room."

They started down the stairs. "We'll play five-card stud —nothing wild. High hand bets. Table stakes. No check raises."

Vern continued reciting the basics as they descended to the game room.

"Three of a kind beats two pair. A straight beats three of a kind. A royal flush beats everything."

On the bottom step, he stopped. A sudden thought astonished him. It was what Junior had said last night when they were looking at the old snapshots—that Pap wasn't in the pictures but was still part of them.

That was true of his dad—right now. Vern had not played poker since his dad died, and yet as he explained the game to Michael his dad's image rose up in his mind as distinctive and powerful as an atomic cloud.

"Are you going to play or not?" Michael asked.

Vern blinked. "Oh, yes."

He crossed the marbleized vinyl floor. He settled himself on a card table chair and hooked his feet behind the chair legs.

He began shuffling the cards, flat on the table, the way his dad did.

"Don't change the expression on your face when you look at your hole card," he said as he began to deal. "It'll ruin your odds."

A Blossom Farewell

JUNIOR WAS PACKING HIS PAPER BAG AGAIN. AT LAST HE was going to spend the night with Mary. At last he was going to be something he had thought he would never be again—happy.

In one half hour he would be walking with Mary through the valley. He and Mary would pass through forests of hemlock and pines, over slopes thick with ferns, beside the high rock walls of the waterfall. It was a dream come true.

Mary would be in front with her cane. He would be behind with his stick. It was amazing the way the forest and bushes seemed to part for Mary, like something out of the Bible.

His mom looked in the door of his room. "Are you ready?"

"Almost," Junior called cheerfully. "Did I tell you about her vultures, Mom?"

"Only two dozen times."

"But vultures aren't supposed to be beautiful and these are. I wish you could come with me and see them."

"Maybe I will some other time."

Junior glanced into his paper bag suitcase and checked the contents. The bag was new, but the contents were the same, except for the picture of him and his dad in each other's hats. He wanted Mary to see that.

Satisfied, he folded the bag and tucked it under his arm. "I'm going to wait on the porch."

"I'll wait with you," his mother said.

Maggie and Ralphie sat on the fence behind the barn. Ralphie had not seen Maggie smile in a long time. It had been so long that he couldn't remember how she looked when she did smile.

"Are you glad you're going on the rodeo circuit this summer?" he asked finally.

"Not really."

"I thought you liked being a trick rider."

"I did."

She sighed, then she shrugged her shoulders. "My mom's got a boyfriend," she explained. "He's a bull rider and his name's Cody Gray. He goes around in a silver Cadillac convertible and thinks he's big time."

"You don't like him?"

"That's not the point."

"What is the point?"

She shook her head. "It's too hard to explain."

"You could try."

"Ralphie"—she turned to face him—"the truth is that my mom has never grown up."

"Listen, you're talking to somebody whose mom runs around in clown suits carrying balloons!"

140

Maggie smiled. It was not the grin Ralphie remembered, but it was better than nothing.

"I mean, Ralphie, she still wants the same things she wanted when she was eighteen years old. She says we're just going back on the circuit this one last summer and then we'll settle down for sure. Maybe she even believes it."

"But you don't."

"I guess I've heard it too many times before," Maggie said. She leaned back against the fence.

"You know, Ralphie," she went on, "the people who are lucky grow up when they're supposed to, not too fast, not too slow—on schedule. The people who aren't lucky—well, they either never grow up, like my mom, or they grow up too fast." She closed her eyes.

"Like you?"

She nodded.

Ralphie glanced down at his artificial leg. "I probably fall into the too-fast category myself."

Maggie opened her eyes and gave him an understanding look. Then she straightened.

"Only, Ralphie, this time I'm going to see that it happens. I'm going to see that we do open a riding school. I'm going to see that we settle down whether my mom likes it or not. This is a Blossom promise to myself. I'm going to take over this family if I have to."

"Mutiny!" Ralphie said.

"Exactly!" Maggie answered.

Ralphie squinted down at Maggie as if he were trying to stare right into her mind. To divert him, she grinned. This grin was more like he remembered.

"I wrote you a postcard," she said.

"Did you? I never got it."

"I never mailed it."

"Well, that explains why I never got it. So what did it say? I'm interested."

"Oh, it was just the ordinary everyday boring miss-you, wish-you-were-here postcard. I had to throw it away though. There was one word that ruined it."

"What word?"

Maggie looked at him out of the sides of her eyes. "Well, the word was not 'love' if that's what you're thinking."

"That's exactly what I'm thinking," Ralphie said. "I know you love me, Maggie. Why else would you ask me to smuggle your dog into the hospital? Why else would you climb up a tree with me? Why would you let me kiss you? You love me and you know it."

Maggie's only answer was that wide pointed-tooth grin.

Vicki Blossom and Junior sat in the swing together. Junior had his paper bag suitcase on his lap. Mud lay at their feet.

Junior said, "Mom?"

She glanced at her watch. "It's now two minutes to ten."

"That wasn't what I was going to ask. I was going to pay you a compliment."

"Be my guest, Junior," Vicki Blossom said.

"Well, I was just going to compliment you on being a good mother."

"Why, Junior."

Junior nodded wisely.

"I don't know," she said. "I'm not exactly like the mothers on Mother's Day cards."

142

"I think you are. No other mother in the world would have helped us smuggle Mud into the hospital."

"Well, that's probably true," she said.

"Or turn the Green Phantom into a success."

"Thank you, Junior. Anyway, I love you as much as the mothers on—" She broke off. "Here she comes. There's Mary."

Vicki Blossom got out of the swing at the same time Junior did. The deserted swing jerked crazily on its chains.

Mud got instantly to his feet.

Vicki Blossom waved to Mary. "Hello! Junior is so excited about spending the night with you. I hope he's not going to be any trouble."

"No trouble at all," Mary said.

"See, Mom, I told you."

Junior's face was lit up like a lamp. He ran down the steps. Mud ran ahead of Junior, mistakenly thinking Junior was headed for the car. Mud stopped at the car door and let out a sharp, insistent bark.

"Not yet, Mud, not yet," Vicki Blossom said. "Saturday."

Junior ran across the yard and into Mary's arms. "How's your grandfather?" she asked.

"Fine!" He was so happy he almost said, "How's yours?" He stopped himself in time.

Mary held him against her for a moment, and then they started to walk toward the woods.

"There's been one good thing about all the rain, Junior," Mary said.

"What?"

"It's done wonders for my wild garden. The poke greens are up. The—"

Junior glanced up at her in alarm. "Aren't we having varmint stew?" Greens were one of Junior's least favorite foods.

"Yes, we are. Yesterday afternoon I had a tug of war with the vultures over one of the finest possums I ever saw on a road. It hadn't been run over more than ten minutes before me and the vultures spotted it."

"Who won the tug of war?" Junior asked.

"It was a tie. We shared. The vultures got the insides. I got the meat."

That was Junior's kind of story. Suddenly Junior remembered his mom on the porch. He turned. She was still standing on the top step with one arm around the banister, watching him.

"Good-bye," he called. He couldn't see the rest of them —Maggie was in the pasture with Ralphie and Dump, Vern was at Michael's house, Pap was in the hospital, Mud was out of sight behind the car—but for some reason Junior called, "Good-bye, Everybody!"

"Good-bye, Junior," his mom called back.

Junior turned. With Mad Mary's arm around his shoulders, he disappeared into the woods.

About the Author

Betsy Byars's sharp perceptions and skill at penetrating the inner life of children have made her one of America's most popular and honored writers for young people. In 1970 her *Summer of the Swans* won the Newbery Medal, and her first book for Delacorte Press, *The Night Swimmers,* won the American Book Award for juvenile fiction in 1980.

A Blossom Promise completes the highly acclaimed Blossom Family Quartet, of which the first three titles are *The Not-Just-Anybody Family, The Blossoms Meet the Vulture Lady,* and *The Blossoms and the Green Phantom.*

Ms. Byars is a licensed pilot and lives in Clemson, South Carolina.

About the Illustrator

Jacqueline Rogers has illustrated the Blossom Family Quartet and many other books for young readers. She lives in West Redding, Connecticut.

BYARS, BETSY   11/17/87
A BLOSSOM PROMISE
(9) 1987 F J BYA
0605   03 366914 02 5   (IC=1)

$13.95

DATE			

NORTHPORT PUBLIC LIBRARY
NORTHPORT, NEW YORK

© THE BAKER & TAYLOR CO.